BECKETT

LANTERN BEACH BLACKOUT: THE NEW RECRUITS, BOOK 3

CHRISTY BARRITT

COMPLETE BOOK LIST

Squeaky Clean Mysteries:

Lantern Beach Romantic Suspense

Tides of Deception

Shadow of Intrigue

Storm of Doubt

Winds of Danger

Rains of Remorse

Torrents of Fear

Lantern Beach P.D.

On the Lookout

Attempt to Locate

First Degree Murder

Dead on Arrival

Plan of Action

Lantern Beach Escape

Afterglow (a novelette)

Lantern Beach Blackout

Dark Water

Safe Harbor

Ripple Effect

Rising Tide

Lantern Beach Guardians

Hide and Seek

Cape Corral Keeper

Seagrass Secrets

Driftwood Danger

Carolina Moon Series

Home Before Dark

Gone By Dark

Wait Until Dark

Light the Dark

Taken By Dark

Suburban Sleuth Mysteries:

Death of the Couch Potato's Wife

Fog Lake Suspense:

Edge of Peril

Margin of Error

Brink of Danger

Line of Duty

Cape Thomas Series:

Dubiosity

Disillusioned

Distorted

Standalone Romantic Mystery:

The Good Girl

Suspense:
Imperfect
The Wrecking

Sweet Christmas Novella:
Home to Chestnut Grove

Standalone Romantic-Suspense:
Keeping Guard
The Last Target
Race Against Time
Ricochet
Key Witness
Lifeline
High-Stakes Holiday Reunion
Desperate Measures
Hidden Agenda
Mountain Hideaway
Dark Harbor
Shadow of Suspicion
The Baby Assignment
The Cradle Conspiracy
Trained to Defend
Mountain Survival

Nonfiction:

Characters in the Kitchen

Changed: True Stories of Finding God through Christian Music (out of print)

The Novel in Me: The Beginner's Guide to Writing and Publishing a Novel (out of print)

CHAPTER ONE

SAMANTHA REYNOLDS GRASPED her leg and moaned.

As her fingers brushed the skin near her heel, she searched for signs of a break beneath the swollen surface. She didn't think her ankle was fractured, but her ligaments definitely felt sprained. She couldn't put any pressure on her foot without flinching and sinking back to the floor.

Had the man who'd left her in this isolated tower deliberately injured her? Had this been one more scheme to ensure she didn't try to leave? She'd hoped her ankle would heal some in the three days she'd been trapped here.

Because there was no way Sami could escape in this state.

She bit back a cry and leaned against the stone wall behind her as doubt nibbled away at any remaining sense of peace.

Stay positive, Sami. Don't let despair win. You'll never survive if you do.

She just wished she didn't feel so clammy and achy.

She was getting sick. The drafty space and the cool nights were making her battered body break down as the moments stretched by.

At least she still had three protein bars. She could ration them for a few more days. But her water would be gone after tomorrow.

In other words, she was running out of time.

She hobbled to her feet and limped to the window. Two narrow openings stretched on opposite sides in the turret, and neither had glass to block the elements.

She cringed as she leaned her head out and stared at the miles of uninhabited mountains.

A burst of wind flung a smattering of dry leaves and small sticks around her. The air almost felt angry as it whistled across the space. Her prison would offer her some shelter but not enough.

If only she could escape . . . but it was a thirty-foot drop to the ground below. Though the walls were made of river rock, they were unscalable—especially with her injured ankle.

The only other way out was through the hatch on the floor. A thick bar probably stretched across the opening on the other side. Sami had broken every fingernail as she'd tried to pry the covering open.

She appeared to be in some type of abandoned castle.

Yes, a castle.

It didn't make any sense. She was in the mountains. In Georgia. At least, that's where she *thought* she was.

Nothing made sense. Because that was all Sami had tried to do since she'd been left here—to make sense of this.

That's what people hired her to do. To untangle the emotional entanglements in their lives and make them orderly, manageable.

Treatable.

But now Sami was incapable of doing that for herself.

As another burst of wind swept through the space, she glanced at the horizon.

The dark clouds in the distance quickly marched toward her.

More despair tried to well in her.

No, Sami. Don't think like that. Somebody will find you.

But how? What if she died up here? Slowly? All alone? Suffering?

Another cry caught in her throat.

Before she could indulge in her fear, a flash of lightning cut through the sky.

Her gaze skimmed the horizon. Not only were the clouds coming in fast, they were turbulent. Shifting. Almost . . . swirling.

At that thought, thunder crashed.

Before she'd been abducted, forecasters had warned about a line of severe storms coming through the area later in the week.

Storms that may even spawn some tornados.

Was that this system?

Another flash of lightning split the sky, and thunder rumbled with ominous warning.

If a tornado came this way . . . there would be no way Sami could take shelter. She was at one of the highest points around. She'd be a goner.

She closed her eyes. *Please, Lord. Don't let it end this way. Please.*

"THE STORM IS COMING in faster than predicted," Rocco Foster's voice came through Beckett Jones' earpiece.

Beckett gripped the handles of his ATV and continued to charge down the mountain path. "I can make it a little further," Beckett said above the roar of his engine.

He was so close to completing the search of his grid area. He didn't want to turn back now. Not until his mission was complete.

"If conditions get bad, you need to find shelter. Forecasters are saying this system is no joke. The tornado that destroyed the town in Arkansas? It came from this system."

Beckett had heard that also. But he hadn't come this far just to give up. He felt certain the rest of his team agreed.

As if to offer confirmation, Axel Hendrix said, "I'm going to keep looking until I have to stop."

"Same here," Gabe Michaels said.

Beckett continued forward on his ATV, his body bouncing as the vehicle hit rocks and roots jutting from the mountain path. It was the easiest way to search this terrain.

They'd gotten intel that the daughter of a federal judge might be in this area.

The woman—psychologist Samantha Reynolds —had gone missing three days ago. Though the FBI was working on the case, Samantha's father had hired Blackout, a private security group, to search for her also. To say Justice Reynolds was sick with worry about his daughter would be an understatement.

Beckett thought the man would have gotten a ransom note by now. But he hadn't.

That was what made this even stranger.

Instead, someone had left a trail of clues to help Blackout find her. Pieces of hair. A rock. Coordinates.

Each were left at crime scenes. Two people had been murdered, and they were somehow connected to this whole mess.

Using those clues, Beckett and his team had been able to pinpoint an area within a ten-mile radius in the Georgia mountains.

With every moment that passed, the chances of Samantha being found alive decreased. That was why they couldn't give up now.

As Beckett's ATV bounced along the trail, the warm breeze shifted to a cold wind that swept over him.

He frowned.

The sudden drop in temperature could only mean trouble.

At that thought, the sky opened up and hail began pelting him.

Beckett ducked, trying to avoid a hit in the face.

But he didn't slow as he moved forward.

"You guys getting knocked in the head by balls of ice?" Gabe asked.

Beckett's teammate was at least four miles away on another part of the search grid they'd drawn up.

"It's hailing here too, and the temperature has dropped by fifteen degrees," Axel said.

"I mean it, guys," Rocco said. "If you need to find shelter, find shelter."

But Beckett wasn't ready to do that yet. Not when he could still keep going down this path. Besides, there was nowhere to take shelter out here. Only hills and slopes.

Lightning cracked then thunder rumbled overhead.

Just as quickly as the hail started, the burst stopped.

Five seconds later, the skies seemed to change channels, and rain began pouring down.

Beckett kept pressing forward.

"I found a cave," Axel said into the comm. "I'm

going to hunker down until the worst of this passes. I can't even see where I'm going, and there are too many steep drop-offs near me for my comfort."

"Keep your eyes on the river in case it rises," Rocco said.

Beckett could hardly hear them over the downpour.

He didn't want to, but he might have to pull over also. He could barely see his tires in front of him as a thick liquid poured from the sky.

That wasn't good, especially in these mountains where cliffs appeared from nowhere. Where landslides were common. Where the ground could wash away beneath him.

Just as those thoughts crossed his mind, the clouds seemed to pause and suck in a breath.

As they did, Beckett spotted something ahead of him.

Was that . . . a castle?

Out here? In the Georgia mountains?

What sense did that make?

Regardless, the place would offer shelter.

It was also somewhere Sami might be kept.

Beckett's heart pounded into his ears at the thought.

He sped forward, knowing he had no time to waste.

He'd check this place out, look for Sami, and get away from the storm for a few minutes.

He prayed for the best . . . even as he prepared for the worst.

CHAPTER TWO

AS RAIN CREPT in through the window openings and puddled on the floor, Sami huddled against the wall.

The storm clouds consumed her. She felt like a bird that had been swept up in the currents of air, unable to break free.

When the rain let up for a moment, Sami pulled herself up just enough to glance outside. She spotted a four-wheeler down below.

Her breath caught.

Was someone here?

She started to yell when the sound caught in her throat.

What if it was the person who'd brought her here?

She didn't remember his face. If that ATV belonged to the FBI or police, wouldn't there be more vehicles? Wouldn't the ATV look more official?

The questions pounded in Sami's head.

But it didn't matter. Whoever had been on the vehicle must now be inside.

"Hello? Can you hear me? Help me!"

But thunder muffled her voice.

As torrents of rain began pouring again, Sami slipped away from the window.

Lightning flashed before the air went still.

Eerily still.

A shiver raked through Sami as her gaze skimmed the green-tinged horizon.

Her breath caught.

Those clouds . . . they were definitely spinning.

A peak dropped below the churning clouds.

It was a funnel cloud, she realized.

A tornado was trying to form.

Sami tried to swallow, but a knot had formed in her throat.

She was helpless to do anything but wait this out.

BECKETT STEPPED inside the old stone building and waited a few seconds for his eyes to adjust to the darkness.

"Hello?"

Just as he expected, there was no answer.

He strode deeper into the building, his footsteps echoing across the stone floor.

What kind of place was this?

The insides weren't exactly a castle. Maybe the basic components were. But old, ratty furniture was scattered around the room, taking away any type of ambience. Based on the dust and sheets that covered various tables and chairs, this place hadn't been used in years.

"Beckett, where are you?" Rocco's voice cut into the silence.

Beckett took another step, adrenaline pumping through his blood as he braced himself for trouble. "I found an old building that looks like a castle. I came inside for shelter and to make sure that Sami isn't here."

"I see a funnel cloud in the distance," Rocco said. "You need to hunker down."

A funnel cloud? Beckett had been in a lot of dangerous situations but never a tornado.

Tension threaded across his shoulders. "I'll stay here until the storm passes."

"Be careful. Until we know exactly what's going on and who's behind it, watch your six."

"Roger that."

He pulled a flashlight from his belt and shone it around the space. Dust particles floated in the beam as he swung the light across the floor. He paused when a staircase across the room came into view.

As the wind blew again, the walls whispered. The breeze stirred up the scents of mildew and dirt, and, for a minute, Beckett felt as if he'd stepped back in time to an ancient, medieval civilization.

"Hello?" he called again into the darkness.

Only the wind and rain answered.

He continued forward, his light bouncing off the walls and into every corner.

Nothing suspicious caught his eye.

Beckett strode closer to the stairway in the distance.

As he reached it, he shined his flashlight onto each stair.

At one time, dirt covered these steps. But the dust at the center of each had been disturbed.

That could mean someone had been up here recently.

It was worth checking out.

Though Beckett had seen no evidence that anyone was inside, he pulled out his gun, just to be safe.

On the second floor, a hallway stretched in front of him. Going room by room, he checked out the space and searched for any signs of life.

But he found no one. Just rooms filled with sheet-covered furniture.

He paused in the last bedroom and listened.

The storm had invaded the area, swarming on top of him now. Even the air felt different, as if it knew something he didn't.

He glanced out the window as a continuous crash sounded in the distance.

A train?

His breath caught.

Wasn't that what people said a tornado sounded like?

When he saw the swirling mass out the window, he sucked in a breath.

That was *definitely* a tornado.

It had touched down less than a half mile away, if he had to guess.

By his estimation, that beast was headed right toward him.

Beckett didn't know if anybody else was in this castle or not.

But he needed to figure that out.

Now.

He quickly searched the rest of the second floor before heading up the final flight of stairs.

When he reached the landing at the top, a trapdoor stretched above him. He tried to move the board strung across it, but it was stuck.

Instead, he grabbed his flashlight and banged on the wooden hatch. "Anyone up there?"

The roar of the storm answered him.

He banged once more, but there was still nothing.

It looked like Samantha Reynolds wasn't here after all.

Now Beckett needed to get back downstairs before this whole building went down and buried him alive.

CHAPTER THREE

WAS THAT ...?

Sami's breath caught.

Had somebody banged on the hatch?

She'd barely heard it over the roar of the storm.

Using her last bit of strength, she sprang on top of the door. Her fists pounded into the wood, each move fraught with desperation. "Hey! I'm here. Help me. Please!"

She waited, desperate for some kind of affirmation. Or to hear the latch being pulled out of place so she could be freed. So she might be safe.

But she heard nothing.

Despair seemed to crack the bubble of hope that had filled her chest. She sagged against the floor as the situation broke her spirit.

Had she been hearing things?

But there was an ATV outside. Somebody was *definitely* here.

Her hair swirled around her as the storm strengthened.

Then she heard a roar. Not the roar of the wind. Not a crack of lightning.

This sound was different.

It was almost like . . . a waterfall was moving over her.

She sucked in a breath.

That funnel cloud had touched down, hadn't it?

Sami couldn't bring herself to look outside.

She didn't need to see with her eyes what her mind already knew.

She was in serious trouble.

"Are you there?" a deep voice called.

Her breath caught.

Someone was down there!

"I'm up here!" she yelled, desperate to be heard over the storm.

"I'm trying to open this door," a muffled voice said. "Watch out."

As she heard something move, Sami scooted back.

Finally, the hatch rose—just barely.

More rain sprayed through the windows, and the rumble outside became even louder.

They didn't have much time.

In the distance, something snapped.

Wood.

Trees.

Her throat went dry as she imagined the swirling funnel cloud destroying the forest.

Finally, the door flew open and a man's head appeared.

"Samantha Reynolds?"

Her heart pounded harder. "It's me."

"Come on. The tornado is going to hit here any second now."

She dragged herself forward, flinching with pain at the throbbing in her ankle. "I'm . . . hurt."

"I've got you."

In one motion, the man lifted her over his shoulder and began trudging down the steps. As he did, the trap door above them slammed shut with the wind.

Darkness surrounded them as they descended the turret, and the whole building shook.

Sami fought the fear trying to claim her.

Help hadn't arrived just in time only for them both to succumb to the elements, right?

The man silently carried her. Talking was a luxury. Movement meant life.

Another sound filled the air. A rumble.

But different than thunder. More dangerous. More aggressive.

She held her breath.

The tornado was eating away at these walls.

The man picked up his pace.

The next instant, they were at the bottom of the stairs.

Moving quickly, he opened a large wooden door and slipped into what appeared to be a closet.

He placed Sami in the corner before crouching over her.

She buried her head against his chest as the world around them was destroyed.

BECKETT FELT his surroundings being ripped apart.

They were directly in the path of the tornado, weren't they?

The woman in his arms whimpered. All he could do was shelter her with his body. But if this castle came down, neither of them would survive that kind of destruction.

Dear Lord, help us now.

Praying was the only thing that might get him through this. Beckett felt certain of that fact.

The wind raged. Objects crashed. The walls trembled.

Beckett may have fought wars overseas, but he'd never experienced anything like this.

The whole place quivered, even the ground beneath him.

Would this entire building be demolished? Would Beckett and the very person he'd come to save be destroyed by the storm?

He prayed that wasn't the case.

He continued to hold this woman.

Samantha Reynolds.

He hadn't had time to observe her for long, but he'd seen enough to know he'd found their missing woman.

She looked just like her pictures—pretty, preppy, and pompous—if not a little haggard because of the circumstances.

If he hadn't gotten to her right when he did . . .

His gut clenched. He didn't want to think about it. Didn't want to think about why someone had abducted her and left her in a turret in the middle of the forest.

There would be time for that later.

Right now, he tightened his embrace on her, trying to protect her from the debris tumbling around them.

These walls were made of stone, not wood. Beckett hoped that would work to their advantage.

But as those very walls shook, he wondered if the dense rocks would end up killing them instead of protecting them.

CHAPTER FOUR

SAMI KEPT her face buried in the stranger's chest.

She didn't have time to think. Only to react.

She needed safety, and he offered that protection.

Everything shook around them. These stone walls were going to collapse, weren't they?

Sami didn't even want to think about what that might be like.

But then, shortly after the violent shaking had begun, it ended.

She froze, wondering if she was missing something. Wondering if the sounds and noises would start again.

Could this be over? Or was she imagining things, letting her optimism get the best of her?

As if to answer her, the walls rumbled again.

Then everything went still.

She remained frozen another minute until she finally loosened her grip on her rescuer.

She drew in a few ragged breaths, trying to compose herself.

Sami squinted in the darkness. She couldn't even see the man who had carried her down the stairs.

Right before he'd picked her up, she had glimpsed a square face with light brown hair and a beard. She knew from the way he carried her that he was strong, tall, and fit.

She knew from burying her face in his chest that he smelled like leather and exhaust fumes—probably from that ATV.

But all she really needed to know was that he'd saved her.

"Are you okay?" His voice rang out through the inky air.

That's when Sami realized she was still clinging to him.

She willed herself to let go.

But she couldn't.

She feared if she did that the darkness might consume her and she'd be all alone again.

"I think I'm okay." Her voice trembled as the words emerged. "My ankle is sore. I can't walk."

"We'll get that checked as soon as we get out of here." He paused. "It sounds like the storm has passed. Let me assess the damage."

The thought of getting out of here, onto that ATV, and riding to safety made hope spring to life inside her again.

"Who are you?" Maybe Sami should have asked that sooner.

"I'm Beckett Jones, and I work for a private security agency called Blackout. Your father hired us to find you."

Her heart pounded in her chest. Her father. Of course.

He would do anything to protect her. Sami had no doubt about that.

"I'm familiar with Blackout. My friend, Elise, lives there on Lantern Beach with her husband. I've visited her there before." She paused before muttering, "Thank you . . . for everything."

"Don't thank me yet. I'm going to stand up, okay?"

"Okay," she muttered.

A moment later, a rattle filled the darkness, and Beckett muttered something beneath his breath.

"What is it?" Sami pressed herself against the wall, sensing bad news was coming.

"I can't open the door. Something must have fallen in front of it and trapped us in here."

Sami bit back another gasp.

They were buried in the rubble in the middle of nowhere . . . how would they ever get out?

BECKETT PUSHED on the door again. But it was no use.

It wouldn't budge.

At least the storm was over. He was thankful for that.

He pressed on his comm to talk to his team.

But nothing happened.

He pulled the battery pack from his belt and felt the casing. The sharp, protruding edges indicated it had been smashed.

He frowned. That must have happened as he escaped the tornado.

He hoped and prayed the rest of his team was okay—and that they'd find him.

He ran his hands over the walls and floor, trying to figure out this space. He would have used his flashlight, but he must have dropped it when he'd gone down the steps with Sami.

Best he could tell, the empty space was approximately four by three feet. Most likely, they were in a closet.

The only thing he could do right now was to wait for his friends to arrive.

He lowered himself back to the floor beside Samantha. As he did, she let out a soft moan beside him.

"Are you comfortable enough, Samantha?" Beckett wished he could see her face. That he could look into her eyes and determine how she was really doing.

He had no idea what had happened between the time she was abducted and now. He could only imagine it was horrific.

"Everyone calls me Sami," she said. "And I'm better now than I was twenty minutes ago."

But her voice didn't sound confident. She was clearly scared.

Were her teeth chattering?

It was no wonder. She'd only been wearing a tank top and shorts when Beckett found her in that tower, *and* she was soaking wet. That wasn't to mention how cold this room was.

"Listen, I know you don't know me," he murmured. "But this is no time to be polite. You need to sit closer. You've got to stay warm so you don't become hypothermic. It's a matter of survival."

He would offer her a jacket or a blanket if he had one. But he didn't.

"I guess . . . that makes . . . sense." But her teeth still chattered.

Beckett scooted closer, wrapped an arm around her, and pulled her to him. She stiffened a moment before finally leaning into him.

"Do you know who left you here?" Beckett kept his voice level as he prodded for information. In situations like these, there was no time to waste. As soon as the two of them were rescued, Beckett and his team needed to continue to search for the person who'd kidnapped her.

The woman felt soft in his arms, like she'd gone limp. Her damp hair brushed his skin, reminding him that she was indeed a real person with real feelings. He shouldn't have made a snap judgment about her.

He'd just assumed that someone like Sami, who'd come from affluence, would be stuck up and spoiled. He didn't get any of those vibes from her now.

While they were trapped together, Beckett might as well learn what he could. Plus, talking would be good for both of them. It would distract them from the dire situation.

"I have no idea who left me here." Her voice sounded strained. "I didn't see his face."

"How did he bring you here?"

She sniffled. "I was getting into my car after the gym when I heard footsteps behind me. The next thing I knew something covered my head and everything went black. When I woke up, I was here."

Beckett's gut clenched. He didn't like the sound of that.

"How did you hurt your ankle?" he asked.

"It must have happened while I was blacked out," she said. "I wondered if the person who abducted me slammed my ankle into something when he carried me up into that turret."

"Even though you didn't see the face of the person who brought you here, do you have any idea who it might be? Has anyone threatened you or acted strangely toward you lately?"

"Not really."

What exactly was going on here? Beckett didn't know, but he didn't like the sound of it either. They were dealing with a sick, dangerous man.

He sensed that this conversation wasn't helping Samantha's anxiety and decided to change the subject.

"So, Sami, you said you're friends with Elise?" he asked instead.

Elise was the wife of Colton Locke, the cofounder and leader of Blackout. She'd come to them about what had happened, acting as their connection to this operation.

"Elise and I went to college and graduate school together," Sami said. "She's one of my dearest friends."

Like Sami, Elise was a psychologist. She used her skills now to help with an organization called Hope House, which was a retreat for former military personnel who were struggling to adjust to life back as civilians.

"That explains why she's been worried sick about you," Beckett told Sami.

"I don't want her to be worried about me, especially since she's pregnant."

"She's a strong woman. She'll be bouncing off the walls when she hears we found you."

"If we get out of here." Another tremble raked through Sami.

"We will. My team will find us."

"Your team?" Her voice lilted with confusion—and maybe a touch of hope.

"That's right. There are three other guys out searching with me. We split up to cover more ground. The storm system came in faster than forecasted."

Silence stretched a moment, filled only with the faint sound of the wind and the occasional tumble of stone.

Finally, Sami said, "I'm sorry that you're trapped here with me."

"Sorry? I'm the one who decided to come. There's no blame here. Now we just need to wait."

"I'm so cold," she muttered.

Beckett put his hand on her forehead.

She was burning up. He had to keep Sami warm until help arrived.

And he needed to keep her thoughts occupied as well.

CHAPTER FIVE

SAMI'S HEAD SWIRLED. She needed to talk. To do something to prevent lethargy from consuming her.

As she rested her head on Beckett's chest, she murmured, "Tell me about yourself."

She needed to keep her thoughts occupied. Otherwise, they might go to dark places. Hopeless places.

Beckett shifted beside her, his muscular arms still holding her close. "About me? I'm from Alabama. I like long walks on the beach, reading books beneath trees, and playing fetch with my dog."

"Really?" His answer was unexpected, to say the least.

"No. I thought it sounded good." Amusement tinged his voice.

"You're strong, brave, *and* funny," Sami said. "I'll make a mental note of that. How did you end up in Lantern Beach working for Blackout?"

"I was a Navy SEAL. Several members of my team decided to get out of the service around the same time. We all ended up working for Blackout."

A Navy SEAL . . . this wouldn't be a good time to mention that Sami loved every Navy SEAL movie she'd ever watched. She'd even watched some of them multiple times.

No one ever expected that about her. Sami was too level-headed to give in to those kinds of whimsies.

Every study she'd ever read pointed to the fact that she should never date someone who was her opposite—someone like this man who relied on his muscles instead of his brains. Well, of course, he relied on his brains too. But he was a warrior by nature.

One day, if she ever got married, it would be to someone who used words and thoughts instead of muscles to help shape the culture.

But, still, there was something undeniably attractive about men like Beckett.

"Why did you want to be a SEAL?" She pressed into him, desperate for warmth. The scent of his leathery cologne brought her a surprising comfort, even in the midst of this turbulent situation, as did his steady heartbeat. "Did you want to save the world?"

"Maybe not the world. But a few people in the world a little at a time."

"It sounds like a noble goal."

"I like to think so." Another shiver rushed through her, followed by an all-over ache. It was almost like her body was at war with itself.

"Usually people in positions like yours can be reckless. That's part of the reason they take jobs like becoming a SEAL. They're risk-takers." Why was she saying this? She wasn't sure. Yet she couldn't seem to stop.

"Is that right?"

"Absolutely. Then when they get back to the States, they miss those bursts of adrenaline. It's the only way they know to operate. That's why they do stupid stuff like jumping into high-risk relationships, riding motorcycles, and taking unnecessary gambles. It's called a sensation-seeking personality."

"It sounds like you've thought about this a lot."

"Give me more time, and I'll uncover everything

that happened in your childhood that led you to this point."

"Now you're the one who's funny," he muttered.

"And you have a very muscular chest."

He let out a rumbling chuckle.

What had Sami just said? She wasn't sure. Had her words slurred?

Her fever must be kicking in.

"We're going to be okay, Sami," Beckett murmured.

He had a way of assuring her that made her actually want to believe it.

As those thoughts wafted through her head, she drifted out of consciousness.

"SAMI?" Beckett shook the woman in his arms.

She didn't stir.

His heart pounded harder in his chest.

Had she blacked out?

He put his hand on her forehead again.

She was burning up even more than before. Her fever must have spiked.

If help didn't find them soon . . . Beckett didn't want to think about what that might mean. He wished he had something to help her. Medicine. Water. Anything.

Dear Lord, please help her!

Just as the thought went through his head, a noise sounded outside.

Was his team here? Or had the person who'd left Sami here come back? Had he been lingering close, waiting for the right time to return and continue with his plan?

So many unanswered questions surrounded this whole mission. But the person behind these crimes was sick and twisted. Two people were already dead, and he wasn't sure how long Sami would make it without medical help.

Just then, he heard someone yell, "Beckett?"

Was that Rocco?

Gently, Beckett removed his arm from around Sami. Then he stood and leaned toward the door, cupping his hands around his mouth as he yelled, "In here!"

"Beckett? Where are you?"

"I'm in this closet!"

"It's a mess around you," Rocco said. "There's a beam in front of the door and piles of stones everywhere. It's going to take time to dig you out."

"Work fast," he called. "Sami's in here with me,

and she's not doing well. She needs to get to the hospital."

"I'll radio for some backup, see if we can get a helicopter out here. In the meantime, the rest of the team should be here soon. The storm caused a lot of damage. Downed trees have made it nearly impassable for the ATVs."

Beckett had little choice but to wait.

Sitting back down, he lifted Sami into his arms again. He had to keep her warm until help got here.

He prayed it wasn't too late.

CHAPTER SIX

SAMI GRIMACED as she sat in her hospital bed with her ankle elevated. The scent of antiseptic spray mixed with the aroma of the flower bouquets around her and her strong coffee.

Her father had gone to get her another cup from a shop down the road. Hospital coffee just wasn't cutting it. Plus, Sami needed a break. Her father had hovered over her since she'd been admitted, and she needed some breathing room.

It had been three days since she'd been rescued. Sometimes, it felt like weeks had passed. Other times, Sami felt like she'd open her eyes and find herself still up in that tower—especially when she tried to sleep.

After a rescue crew had dug her and Beckett out, Sami had been taken via helicopter to a nearby hospital for treatment. Doctors had given her antibiotics and pain meds for her fever and body aches, and they'd given her a walking boot for her sprained ankle.

Then the FBI had sent Special Agent Marco Sanders to question her. She'd told him everything she knew—which wasn't much. They believed her abduction was tied in with one of her father's cases.

Throughout it all, Sami's thoughts kept going back to the man who'd rescued her.

Beckett Jones.

She wasn't the type to get schoolgirl crushes, but that man had saved her life. He was the definition of a hero. Sami wasn't sure if she'd even told him thank you. Everything was a blur—especially since she'd passed out. Yet those memories would always be burned into her mind.

Her father knocked at the door before stepping into the room, triumphantly holding up a paper cup. "Good news. I've got your favorite coffee, *and* the doctor said that you're going to be able to go home today."

That was good news.

But going home? Sami didn't want to go back to

Atlanta. She wasn't ready for that yet. She wasn't ready to return to life as she'd known it, nor could she mentally handle her job. Not until she sorted out her own trauma.

So what was she supposed to do?

"You can come stay with me." Her dad seemed to read her thoughts as he glanced at her, his brow furrowed with years of wisdom. He had a slight build, pale skin, and a receding hairline.

But Royce Reynolds was one of the best men Sami had ever known—one of the wisest also.

She thought about his offer and tried to find the right words. "But, Dad . . ."

"But what?" He tilted his head, his thinking gaze on her.

That's what people called his unreadable expression. When people tried to get a read on him in court, it was always close to impossible.

In her opinion as a licensed counseling psychologist, a person's gaze said so much more than their expression. Expressions could be faked. But people's eyes always told the truth.

"I'm just going to end up sitting there by myself. You have a lot of work to do, especially with the trial of the century starting soon."

That's what the media was calling the upcoming

court case her father was presiding over. A big tech company, Hemisphere, was being sued for illegally selling people's information to advertisers. To say people's feelings were stirred up about it would be an understatement.

Her dad paused near her bed and handed her the coffee. "But I could see you in the evenings. You'd be safe at my place."

Sami frowned. The FBI still had no idea who had done this to her. The man who'd abducted her was still out there. Still at large.

A shiver raked through her at the thought.

Sami wouldn't have any peace in her life until he was behind bars. Every time she closed her eyes, she was transported back in time. To that cold, lonely tower. To the moment hope had disappeared. When she'd been certain she would die from that wicked tornado.

Her father stepped closer to her bed and frowned. "There's something I haven't told you."

Her lungs tightened at her father's somber tone. "What's that?"

"The man who took you . . . he left clues, almost teasing us that you were within reach yet hidden."

She set her coffee down. "What kind of clues?"

Her father's gaze darkened. "Your hair was found at two different murder sites."

Nausea roiled in her stomach as she realized the extremes this person had gone to plan this out. "Who was killed?"

"People seemingly unrelated to you. With no obvious connection. One was a forty-year-old woman. Single. She had no criminal record. The other was a thirty-five-year-old male."

"How did they die?"

"The woman was smothered in her bed. The man died of a head injury—he was found dead in his backyard. Based on the bruises on his back, it looks like he was pushed from an old treehouse."

"What?" The question came out sounding nearly breathless. But . . . Sami needed to make sense of this. The task felt nearly impossible.

Her father frowned. "It's strange, I know. This person also left numbers written on his victims' hands—another reason we know the man who fell from the tree was murdered. They were the coordinates to the area where you were found."

A chill washed through her. She wished she could enjoy this coffee, but Sami wouldn't be enjoying anything right now. Not knowing what she did.

"Why would he abduct me only to send clues?" She rubbed her arms as she felt goosebumps popping up.

"It sounds like he's playing a game."

Her chill deepened. "A sick game."

Her father straightened, showing his shifting thoughts. "The Blackout team found you and brought you back safely. So I've hired them to further investigate what's going on. I trust they will find the person who did this to you as well. They'll be working separate from the FBI to find answers."

The Blackout team . . . they all seemed very capable.

The whole experience still seemed surreal.

But the fact that Sami had been rescued by a man who'd stepped straight out of her dreams made her want to pinch herself. She'd never forget when they'd been trapped in the closet. Never forget what a rock Beckett had been in the middle of a turbulent situation.

The man wasn't her type—not what she was looking for in a romantic relationship. But he captured her thoughts like no one had in a long time.

She glanced out the window at the summer day. As she did, something caught her eye.

A man stood on the sidewalk . . . staring at her room.

"Sami?"

She glanced at her dad. "That man . . ."

Her father walked to the window. But when Sami looked back, the man was gone.

Gone? Had she been seeing things?

"What man?" her father asked.

She shook her head, a deep chill racing through her veins. "I thought I saw someone out there."

"I don't see anyone . . ." Her father glanced back at her with worry in his gaze.

"My eyes must be playing tricks on me." But Sami didn't believe her own words.

She'd seen that man. It was almost like he'd known Sami was in this room. That he'd wanted to send a message.

It was her abductor, wasn't it? He was letting her know that he wasn't done yet.

She held back a cry.

She had to figure out a plan—now.

At that thought, an idea trickled into Sami's mind. It might sound crazy.

But her plan just might work as well.

Sami picked up her coffee again and took a sip. "I'd like to go visit Elise while I recover."

Her father squinted. "Do you mean in Lantern Beach?"

Lantern Beach was an island in North Carolina where Blackout was located.

Sami nodded, the idea building momentum inside her the more she thought about it. "Elise lives at the Blackout campus. I went there a few months ago, and I loved it. I'm sure Elise wouldn't mind. That way, I'll be at Blackout's disposal. I can answer any questions."

His eyes narrowed with thought until he slowly nodded. "And if you stay on campus with them, you should be safe."

"Exactly."

Her father stared at her another moment, his gaze skimming back and forth with thought. Finally, he nodded. "Sounds like a good idea. But whatever happens, we can't let this man find you again."

Sami's stomach clenched at the worry in his tone. This man finding her again was the last thing she wanted also. But until this guy slipped up and left more clues to his identity, how would they even know how to find him?

She didn't know.

But she hoped the team from Blackout might be able to help her.

"DO we know who that castle belongs to?" Beckett leaned back in his chair as he and the rest of his team met together at the Blackout headquarters in Lantern Beach. "Words I never thought I'd say . . ."

He hadn't encountered too many castles in his time as a SEAL. Cartels, terrorists, even modern-day pirates . . . yes. But never a castle until this case.

He and his team sat around a conference table with cups of coffee in front of them as they formulated their next steps.

His three team members were here along with Colton Locke, the leader of the organization. Three other men also worked for Blackout, but they were out on other assignments right now.

The organization's isolated location on the island offered them privacy—but sometimes that same seclusion put them in life-threatening situations.

No bridges led to the oversized sandbar. Boats and on occasion a helicopter were the only means of getting to the place. If—when—storms came, residents were at the mercy of Mother Nature.

Rocco Foster was their team leader—strong, diplomatic, even-keeled.

Axel Hendrix was the motorcycle-riding, head-turning one of the group.

Gabe Michaels, aka Junior, was the youngest—the rookie, so to speak. The rest of the guys liked to give him a hard time. It wasn't only because of his age. It was also the fact he had a youthful optimism the rest of them had abandoned.

Not that any of them were that old. Beckett was the oldest at thirty-four. But he'd seen enough hard things to fill up several lifetimes. That's how it seemed, at least.

The four of them had worked together uncountable times and had formed a great bond. Mostly over sushi, as they liked to joke.

"The castle belongs to a man named Jim Pfizer." Rocco's British accent rang across the room. "However, Jim died two years ago, and the place was left to his son, John. John now lives out in Montana. I've verified his alibi. He wasn't in Georgia when all this happened."

Beckett frowned. Of course not. That would have been too easy.

"Did you get any type of history on why this guy even built a castle in the first place?" Axel leaned back and narrowed his gaze.

"John said his dad was eccentric and had a lot of

money. He thought it would be fun to build a castle on some property he'd bought out in the mountains. The family used to go there on vacation when he was a child. But then his father developed MS and was unable to get there as much. John eventually plans to sell the place. Of course, now there's not that much to sell."

Beckett remembered looking at the place as he'd ridden away from the wreckage. Most of the stones comprising the building had crumbled. Now the structure looked like ruins from an ancient Scottish clan—definitely not something people expected to see in the Georgia mountains.

But mostly what Beckett remembered was the fear hovering in the air during those final moments. He was so thankful that his life and Sami's life had been spared. It could have been a much different story.

That tornado had been an F4, which was uncommon in the area. Many houses had been lost, but thankfully no lives. None that Beckett had heard of, at least.

"Do we have any suspects?" Gabe twirled the pencil in his hands. His ADD tendencies required him to always move.

"The most likely scenario is that this abduction

probably ties into one of Justice Reynolds' cases," Colton said. "He's a federal judge, and he's been the target of threats on many occasions."

Beckett's lips turned down in a frown as he listened. He hated thinking about that woman being in danger. In fact, he'd been thinking about Sami often in the four days since he'd rescued her.

No doubt, experiences like the one they'd been through had bonded them.

But he wanted to know how she was doing. How she was *really* doing.

She'd clearly hurt her ankle. But he hadn't seen any other injuries before medics had whisked her to the hospital. However, he could only imagine her inner turmoil.

"Is there a way we can find out if the judge has had any specific threats lately?" Axel asked. "So we can figure out some possible motives."

Rocco nodded. "Yes, and that leads me to one other thing . . ."

"What's that?" Beckett asked.

Rocco looked past Beckett, toward the doorway.

"People who hate my father could be trying to send him a very clear message."

Beckett's eyes widened at the soft, familiar voice.

Was that . . .?

He turned around and saw someone unexpected standing at the entrance of the room.

Sami Reynolds.

CHAPTER SEVEN

SAMI CLEARED HER THROAT, suddenly feeling self-conscious as she stood in the doorway of the conference room. She hadn't wanted a dramatic arrival. But she was the best one to answer the question she'd heard thrown out.

"Sami asked if she could come stay here for a couple of weeks as she recovers." Colton stepped beside her. "She wants to do whatever she can to help figure out who did this to her, and she's agreed to answer whatever questions we might have."

As Colton spoke, Sami's eyes traveled to each of the men seated inside the conference room. But her gaze stopped on Beckett.

The man who'd rescued her.

He looked just as handsome as she remembered.

Sami felt her cheeks flush when their gazes met. When she remembered what they'd been through together. When she remembered how safe she'd felt with him.

How vulnerable.

Vulnerability was something she kept locked away. Being guarded served her well as a psychologist. She much preferred talking about scars rather than talking about open wounds.

But her time with Beckett had been all emotion. Unplanned. Raw.

She'd be lying if she said she didn't feel a touch self-conscious about it now. Very few people had ever seen her in that state before.

He offered a quick nod as he sat there. Sami's lips tugged up in a slight smile in response.

Sami hobbled inside and sat in a chair Colton pulled out for her.

Then she turned to the men around her. "I want to find the guy who did this more than anybody. So whatever questions you have for me, I'm more than happy to answer them. My father has given me permission to speak about some of his cases. Although I can't necessarily share all the details, I'll tell you whatever I can."

She hadn't expected to be nervous.

Then again, she hadn't expected to be abducted and kept in a tower of a castle in the mountains of Georgia either.

"Does your father have any inclination about who might be behind this?" a man with a British accent asked. "I'm Rocco, by the way."

Introductions went around the room.

"And, of course, you've already met No-Smile Beckett," Colton said.

"No-Smile Beckett?" She glanced at him.

He shrugged. "Long story."

She looked forward to hearing that later when matters weren't quite as pressing.

"My father doesn't know who's behind this." Sami raised the water bottle she'd brought with her and took a sip. "Most people who threaten him are anonymous. Cowards, I'd say. If you're going to have an opinion, own it."

"I agree." Beckett grabbed a water bottle and twisted off the top. "Don't hide behind a faceless identity."

Satisfaction stretched through Sami at his agreement. She wasn't sure why it caused a rush of contentment, but it did. "His most controversial case right now involves Hemisphere."

"The tech company?" Rocco tilted his head.

Sami nodded. "That's right. They got caught selling people's personal information without permission. Some people think it was an invasion of privacy. Others thought it was a brilliant marketing tactic. My father's gotten hate mail from both sides."

"His ruling could cost the company millions," Rocco said.

"Exactly. And, on the other side, if he decides what the company is doing is okay then others will hold him liable. People like Lawrence Murdock."

Colton shifted in his seat. "Who is Lawrence Murdock?"

"He's a man who's sent threats to my father. He claims my dad is corrupt and being paid off by both politicians and big tech."

"How common are these threats?" Beckett asked.

"Pretty common. My father probably gets fifty or more threats a year. Most of them don't amount to anything. But he's had to hire extra security. With our country's political environment being what it is, he can't take any chances."

Sami heard her phone buzz and glanced at the screen. She frowned when she read the text there.

"Everything okay?" Beckett leaned toward her, that air of protectiveness surrounding him again.

"I just got a text from an unknown number." She stared at the words, trying to make sense of them.

"What does it say?"

"It says, 'Let me in.'"

The guys around the table glanced at each other.

Sami stared at the words again and frowned.

What in the world did that mean?

———

BECKETT DIDN'T KNOW what was going on, but he didn't like the sound of it.

That text supposedly could be random and unrelated.

But they needed to treat it as if it was related.

Let me in. The words sounded vaguely familiar. Or maybe it was just a common phrase. He didn't know.

But unease jostled in his chest.

"If you give us the number, we can attempt to pinpoint the location of the sender," Rocco said. "However, if this is from a burner phone, it may not lead us to any answers."

"Of course." Sami read the number out loud, and Rocco jotted it down.

As she did, Beckett observed her.

Sami looked just as beautiful as he remembered. Her slim build coupled with her long brown hair, big eyes, and heart-shaped face made a very nice picture.

Any friend of Elise's had to be a standup person anyway. Elise was too top-notch to settle for anything else.

Beckett wasn't sure Sami being here was a good idea. However, another part of him felt thrilled. Perhaps it was because of what they'd experienced together. But whenever he looked at Sami or thought about her, a surge of protectiveness swelled inside him.

At least, this way she'd be close. At least, he could keep an eye on her.

Coming here instead of hiding away at her father's house had taken a lot of strength, and wanting to help took courage. Maybe she wasn't totally the spoiled rich woman he'd assumed.

Just then Colton's phone beeped. He looked at it and frowned.

"What is it?" Rocco asked.

"It's Ernie. He just found a package in the middle of the lawn."

"Where did it come from?" Beckett asked.

"That's the weird thing—he doesn't know, nor

does anyone he's talked to. It's wrapped in brown paper, and there's no name on it. He said he hasn't touched it, just in case."

Rocco stood. "I'll go check it out."

Beckett didn't like the sound of that, but he tried not to show his apprehension. Not yet.

Until someone told him otherwise, he would keep trying to find answers for Sami.

He turned toward her. "Have you thought of any personal enemies or adversaries we might need to check out?"

Sami shrugged, her gaze darkening as she stared into the distance with thought. "Not really."

Beckett wondered what it would be like to live without any enemies. In his line of work, that seemed impossible.

Before they could talk more, Colton's phone rang again. After he put it to his ear, he rose to his feet, his shoulders bristled.

"We need to get everybody out of here," he said. "Now."

"What's going on?" Beckett rose as he asked the question.

Colton started toward the door. "Rocco thinks there's a bomb in that package. I need to get Elise. Axel, you're in charge of Sami."

"I'll watch over her," Beckett interjected. "If that's okay."

"In charge of me?" She practically snorted. "That's a bit of an overstatement—"

"That's fine," Colton rushed.

Beckett stood and grasped her arm. "We need to go."

She opened her mouth as if to rebuke the statement but then shut it again.

"Axel, Gabe, I need your help clearing the building. Now." Colton's gaze met everyone else's once more before he hurried from the room.

Was this in some way related to the text message Sami had received?

Beckett wasn't sure. They would figure that out later.

For now, they needed to get out of here.

CHAPTER EIGHT

SAMI HOBBLED TOWARD THE EXIT, moving as fast as she could. But her walking boot served as a handicap.

Urgency zinged through the air as people darted toward the doors in the distance.

Despite her sluggish pace, Beckett remained steadily beside her. He kept his hand on her back as he both urged her forward and kept her steady.

But as the crowd in front of them rushed outside and Sami still lingered a good distance behind the rest, Beckett turned toward her.

"Unfortunately, we've got to get you out of here," he muttered, "faster than this."

The next instant, he scooped her into his arms and took off at a light jog.

Sami had no choice but to let him. She knew she was moving too slowly on her own. The last thing she wanted was to get both of them killed.

"Are you okay?" Beckett didn't sound the least bit winded as he rushed toward the door.

"Slightly embarrassed but okay."

"This is nothing to be embarrassed about."

"That's easy for you to say. You're not the one being carried." She was usually the one who helped others. The one who needed to be strong.

At the moment, she felt helpless. Her listening skills did no good in this situation. However, Beckett's warrior-like abilities would prove to be a lifesaver.

"My first priority is your safety. I need to make sure that whatever is going on, it doesn't affect you." He shoved the door open and stepped into the bright, stifling hot day. The sunshine seemed deceptively cheerful considering the circumstances.

Sami had no choice but to swallow her pride. She couldn't get through this on her own. "I appreciate your help."

Sami also appreciated the solid feel of his chest beneath her. The man was strong. Well-built. He even smelled good.

Why would she notice something like that at a

time like this? It made no sense, even to her analytical brain. Or maybe it made more sense than she wanted to admit.

Either way, it didn't matter right now. Not when lives were on the line.

Finally, they reached an area outside of the gate. Rocco directed everyone farther down the street. Once they were a safe distance away, Beckett placed Sami back on her feet as he observed the area around them.

As he did, the skin on the back of her neck rose.

She glanced around, searching for the source of the feeling. All she saw were some woods and marsh.

What had caused the goosebumps to pop across her skin?

She remembered seeing that man outside the hospital. He'd been watching her there.

Was he watching her here also?

Her head swam at the thought.

"Sami?"

She looked up at Beckett a moment. But she said nothing. Instead, she continued to look around, searching for the source of her discomfort.

All she saw were clusters of people standing on the gravel road.

No one seemed to be watching her.

But that was exactly how she'd felt.

Instinctively, she gravitated closer to Beckett, craving his protection like a soldier might a bullet-proof vest.

"Sami?"

She looked up at Beckett and saw the questions in his gaze. She had to tell him what her gut was telling her. It was only right.

Her throat ached as she said, "I know this might sound crazy. But I'm nearly certain that the person who abducted me has followed me here also."

BECKETT'S GUT clenched as Sami's words rolled over him.

He glanced around, his guard rising with the speed of a steel trap. "Stay close to me."

Even to his own ears, his voice sounded hard and left no room for argument.

Sami stood close enough that her arm brushed against his. He wanted her close enough to touch. That was the only way she'd remain safe.

He scanned everything around them. The woods. The marsh. The crowd. The road.

He searched the shadows between trees. The horizon in the distance.

But nothing out of place caught his eyes.

Was this all a mistake? Or was someone really watching Sami?

As they stood on the road, a balmy summer breeze rushed over them.

Even though the campus mostly housed the Blackout team members and their spouses, support staff also stayed here. The organization had grown quickly and efficiently, and they'd added several new employees in the past year. Two housekeepers, a cook, and a groundskeeper. The security guard, Ernie, stayed off site.

Each group huddled close, speaking with concern in their voices.

They'd all moved far enough away from the campus buildings that the guardhouse was a good quarter mile down the road. The Daniel Oliver Building, with their apartments and offices, couldn't even be seen.

Axel lingered close, on the lookout for trouble around them. Rocco stood behind him, on the phone with someone.

Just then, Gabe cut through the crowd toward them. He'd been in charge of making sure the building was clear.

"Did you hear anything?" he rushed.

Beckett shook his head. "Last I heard, Ty and Colton were investigating. Ty just happened to pull up when all this happened."

Ty Chambers was the co-founder of Blackout and married to the island's chief of police, Cassidy.

"What about Elise?" Alarm filled Sami's voice. "Where is she?"

"She actually went into town, so she's okay."

"Praise God."

Gabe turned back to Beckett. "Ty and Colton pulled out that new robot they're working on and unwrapped the package. It does look like a bomb."

Beckett felt his lungs freeze. That wasn't what he wanted to hear.

Sami let out a muffled cry beside him. Acting on instinct, Beckett lightly placed his hand on her back. As he did, he felt a zing rush through him.

A zing?

This situation was clearly messing with his head.

His thoughts turned back to the news he'd just heard. How had someone managed to sneak a bomb onto their campus?

He didn't like the thought of it.

He remembered the text that had been sent to Sami. *Let me in.*

Had that person texted Sami right before leaving the bomb? If so, what was he trying to prove?

This suddenly didn't seem like such a simple operation. In fact, protecting Sami might turn Beckett's life upside down.

But as the sweet scent of her perfume wafted up to his nostrils, he realized that Sami was worth the risk. The woman intrigued him in ways that she shouldn't.

Not only was Beckett single and content, Sami was nowhere near his type. His type was someone low maintenance. Down-to-earth. Someone who'd be happy with a simple life.

"Have you seen anyone strange lingering near the property?" Beckett asked.

Gabe shrugged. "No. Why?"

"We need to check our security footage. We're also going to need to search these woods and figure out how that bomb got onto our campus. The person who sent it could still be close."

"Ty already called Chief Chambers. She and her guys are headed here now."

"Good. But, right now, the important thing is that we keep everyone safe."

Beckett let out a deep breath and glanced around once more for any signs of trouble.

Before he could say anything else, an explosion rocked the air around them, sending gasps through the crowd and birds scurrying through the air.

His lungs froze.

Ty and Colton . . .

Were they okay?

CHAPTER NINE

SAMI FELT her knees go weak. Before she hit the ground, Beckett grasped her elbows and held her up. But she felt the tremble rake through him also.

That explosion had shaken him. Had any of his friends been hurt?

Please, God ... no.

As another chill washed over her, she scanned the woods, searching for whatever had triggered her earlier reaction. Had triggered that feeling of being watched.

Someone had gotten that bomb into headquarters. Where had this person gone afterward? He couldn't have gotten very far.

Rocco, Gabe, and Axel cut through the crowd, running toward the explosion.

Ty and Colton had been near that bomb.

What if one of them had been hurt? What if this somehow *did* lead back to her? Sami would never forgive herself for coming here and putting these people in danger if that was the case.

She looked at Beckett, her gaze locking on his. "Do you need to go help?"

His jaw tightened as if an internal battle waged inside him. "I'm staying with you."

"But if you need to help your friends . . ."

He shook his head. "I'm not leaving you alone. Not now."

She shuddered. She knew exactly what he was talking about. If it was about her and if her gut feeling was right, then someone was watching her. Targeting her. This person could be waiting for just the right time to make another move.

Sirens sounded in the distance. A moment later, two police vehicles screeched to a halt behind them. A blonde with a growing belly rushed from one of the SUVs toward Beckett.

Cassidy Chambers.

She recognized the police chief. Sami had worked with the woman on a case when she'd been in town last time.

"Where's Ty?" Cassidy hurried.

Beckett tensed beside Sami, and he lowered his voice as he said, "He was on campus."

Without another word, Cassidy darted toward the gate. One of her officers followed behind.

As they did so, another officer strode toward them. Sami glanced at his name badge.

Dillinger.

Concern etched in the knot between the officer's eyes. "Do you know if Ty was near the bomb?"

Beckett rubbed a hand over his beard. "He was. Unfortunately, we don't have an update on the situation."

The officer sucked in a deep breath. "Who did this?"

"We don't know. But whoever is responsible could still be close."

Officer Dillinger stepped away from them and reached for his gun. "I'll check out the woods."

"Good idea. Be careful."

Sami shifted her weight from her injured leg, her discomfort growing. She didn't want to draw any attention to herself or be any trouble. But she wasn't sure how much longer she could stand. Maybe she hadn't progressed as much as she'd thought.

Beckett seemed to sense that as he glanced at her, his observant gaze assessing her. "How about if you lean against one of these police cars? I'm sure they won't mind. If anybody gives you a hard time, direct them to me."

Sami was sure that not many people wanted to be confronted with someone like Beckett, a stoic giant.

He helped her to the police car, and she leaned against the hood, taking some weight off her ankle.

Thank goodness. She already felt better.

If only it was this easy to put her mind more at ease.

But she wouldn't feel at ease until she knew that everybody was okay.

A moment later, Gabe jogged back toward them. "Colton and Ty are fine. They weren't near the bomb when it went off."

Praise God . . .

Beckett glanced around again and, when he spoke, Sami realized her relief was short-lived.

"I wish I could say this was over, but it's not." Beckett narrowed his eyes. "We still have a lot of work to do. We need to be prepared for the possibility that the worst might still be yet to come."

WHILE THE POLICE investigated the scene, Beckett kept an eye on Sami. He wanted to get her away from this area and take her somewhere out of the open. She didn't need to see all this playing out. She'd already been through enough.

Since it was lunchtime, he walked Sami to his truck and they headed to The Crazy Chefette, a local restaurant, to get a bite to eat.

Olivia Rollins, one of the waitresses, greeted them as they stepped inside.

"I didn't think you were working here anymore," Beckett said.

"I fill in on occasion. Mostly so I can get a discount on my food." Olivia winked before raising her eyebrows. "I heard you guys had some excitement at the Blackout campus."

Beckett scooted closer to Sami, his gaze quickly scanning all the patrons inside. The place appeared full of vacationers and families. He saw no one suspicious.

But he'd still keep his eyes wide open, just in case.

He turned back to Olivia. "You talk to Axel?"

"He called to let me know he was okay." Olivia shifted her tray to the other hand. "That could have turned out bad. Really bad."

"You don't have to remind me."

Her gaze moved to Sami. "I'm Olivia."

Sami waved. "I'm Sami. It's great to meet you."

Beckett noted how warm and sincere Sami's voice sounded as she replied to Olivia. She seemed like the type of person who could be friends with anybody. How was it possible for anyone not to like someone like her? She was certainly different than Beckett had first assumed.

Was her friendliness the reason she was targeted? All the evidence pointed to the fact that these crimes were about her father and that Sami was simply a casualty.

"Why don't you guys have a seat over there in the corner." Olivia nodded toward a booth in the distance. "I'll be right over to take your drink orders."

Beckett led Sami to a table, and they sat across from each other.

He was still on edge and waiting for trouble to appear again. He hoped it didn't happen, but he needed to be prepared in case it did. In the meantime, he'd enjoy the scent of sizzling hamburgers and freshly cooked french fries that floated around him.

"I'm glad your friends are okay." Sami picked up the menu and glanced at it.

"Me too." He studied her face a minute. "You really think this is about your father?"

"I don't know. I really felt like someone was watching me right before that bomb went off as well as at the hospital—"

"What?"

She frowned as realization rolled over her features. "I meant to bring it up earlier. But I looked out the window at the hospital, and I'm nearly certain I saw a man outside. He was looking right at my room. I know he couldn't see inside. It was more like he wanted to send a message."

"I don't like the sound of that."

"Me either. I mean, I know my father is the most obvious target, and I know that by hurting me, it would hurt him. But . . . something about this just makes me wonder."

Heaviness stretched between them.

Sami glanced around, her eyes both curious and approving. "Come to this place often?"

"You mean Elise didn't bring you here last time you visited?"

"No, actually she didn't. We had too much fun experimenting with some new recipes. We used to do it all the time in college, so we decided to relive some of those glory days."

Beckett tried to imagine the two of them being so young and carefree. In some ways, that was easy. Both of the women could clearly cut loose and have fun. But, in other ways, too much had happened to imagine those times. Tragedy had marred both of their lives.

"It sounds like the two of you are close," he finally said.

"I love Elise like a sister. I'm so glad she's okay." Sami's smile faded as if worry over what could have happened invaded her thoughts.

"We all are," Beckett said. "That could have turned out much worse. As much as I'd like to just chat right now and take your mind off things, I'm afraid that we don't have that luxury."

The light faded from her gaze. "Anything you want to ask, I'll tell you. As long as I can order food first. And as long as I can ask you questions also. It's kind of what I do for my job. I'm not used to being on the other side of this."

His lips almost wanted to creep up into a smile. But they didn't.

But it was too late. Sami had caught him.

"I get to go first. Why do they call you No-Smile Beckett?"

He shrugged. "The guys and I . . . our way of showing we care about each other is to give each other a hard time."

"But there still has to be a story behind it . . ." She tilted her head and waited.

"I'm incapable of smiling."

Her eyes widened. "Really?"

"No."

She shook her head. "I'm picking up on what you're throwing down."

"What does that mean?"

"You may not smile with your lips, but your eyes dance. They say entirely more than your expression."

He leaned closer. "What are they saying right now?"

"You're thinking I'm full of psychological mumbo jumbo." She cocked her eyebrows again. "Am I right?"

She'd hit the nail on the head, but he didn't want to admit that. Instead, he shrugged. "I would never say that."

The corners of her lips curled up in a smile. "You don't have to. Your eyes say it for you."

He was going to have to be careful around this one. Her words were hitting a little too close to home.

"We should probably order," he finally said, ready to change the subject.

He made a few recommendations to her. When Olivia came back, Beckett ordered a burger and fries, and Sami ordered some jalapeño lemonade and a grilled cheese and peach sandwich.

He made a mental note that Sami had a bit of an adventurous side, based on what she'd picked to eat. He'd assumed she'd been the uptight Type A kind of woman. But he should know better than to jump to conclusions. His initial impression about her had already been proven wrong.

Still, Sami wasn't the only one who liked to figure people out. There was nothing Beckett loved more than standing at the edge of the crowd and watching people. That trait had proven valuable on several operations, especially in his role as a sharpshooter.

"Okay, Beckett." Sami placed her elbows on the table and leaned toward him, not bothering to hide how he had her full attention. "What do you want to know?"

There was so much.

But before the first question could leave his lips, Sami's phone buzzed.

When she glanced down, her face went pale.

Beckett braced himself.

What now?

CHAPTER TEN

SAMI BLINKED as she stared at the message on her screen. Certainly, she wasn't reading the words correctly. But she knew she was.

"Sami?" Beckett's voice stretched across the table.

She couldn't even read the words out loud. Instead, she handed the phone to Beckett so he could see the message himself.

"You should have let me in." Beckett looked up at her, a wrinkle of curiosity between his eyes. "This is from the same number as the other message?"

Sami nodded. "The first message he sent said, 'Let me in.' Now he's telling me I should have let him in. What an odd word choice. Did this guy really text me hoping I'd let him inside the Blackout head-quarters?"

Beckett ran his hand across his jaw. "That's a good question. I agree that something's off about this wording."

Sami's face scrunched as theories pummeled her thoughts. "I didn't let him in so he sends a bomb instead to take out the place? I have to admit—it's my job to sort out the lies from the truth. It's what I do for a living. But this is eluding me right now."

"Something very strange is going on here, and you're clearly the target."

Sami ran her hands over her face, wondering how her life had come to this. She should be at her practice today. She should be meeting with her clients and helping them work through their problems. Progress came through consistency.

Afterward, she was supposed to meet a friend at the gym. They would work out and then clean themselves up before going to try a new restaurant.

Her life back in Georgia was full and complete.

Now, everything had been turned upside down.

She held back a frown at the thought.

Their drinks were delivered, and they both took long sips.

Finally, Beckett spoke again. "You're a psychologist. I know you've examined some of your father's cases. Are there any that stand out besides Lawrence Murdock's? Are there any other threats that you consider valid?"

She was glad he asked because she did have someone she wanted to mention. "There was a man named Clark Stephens. His wife died tragically after she had an adverse reaction to a new medication. Clark sued the company who developed it, and the case made it to federal court. Ultimately, my father ruled in favor of the pharmaceutical company."

"And Clark didn't take it well?"

Sami shook her head. "Not at all. He had to be admitted to the psychiatric ward at a hospital for a while. Last I heard, he was out but clearly not doing well."

"Someone like that could be capable of abducting you and killing others."

Her throat tightened at the blunt reminder about the reality of this situation. "I hate to think about it, but you're right."

"We'll add him to our list."

Their conversation paused as their food was delivered. After chatting for a few minutes, Olivia left, and it was just Sami and Beckett again.

"I hope we can find some answers for you soon,

Sami." Beckett's gaze looked sincere as he stared across the table at her.

His eyes were so expressive that she felt like she could study them all day.

But that would be inappropriate. In fact, she already felt like she stared at him entirely too much.

She glanced away and cleared her throat before saying, "Thank you."

Because the sooner they figured out who was behind this, the sooner Sami could resume her normal life.

And maybe she'd even be able to sleep at night again.

"SO, tell me, Beckett, why did you become a SEAL?"

Beckett watched as Sami leaned back in her seat, waiting for his answer. Her intelligent eyes scrutinized him as if he were a test subject in a new scientific study. The sound of other patrons murmuring around them mixed with the tantalizing scent of seafood and Old Bay seasoning.

He had nothing to hide, so Sami could psychoanalyze him all she wanted. He could already see her wheels turning as she tried to figure him out. As a matter of fact, it was kind of fun to keep her guessing.

He stared at the door in the distance as a family with six kids wandered inside. "I always knew I wanted to be in the military. My father was in the military. My grandfather. My brother. While I was shooting for the stars, I figured I might as well see if I could make it through SEAL training. I did. And I loved every minute of being a SEAL. Almost every moment at least." His voice trailed as flashes from one of their last missions filled his thoughts.

Some things couldn't be redeemed, no matter how someone tried to explain them.

Things like Operation Grandiose.

"So, your family instilled in you a sense of justice and the importance of fighting for what was right." She nodded slowly. "That's good."

For a minute, Beckett felt like he might as well be back in one of his therapy sessions, sessions like the ones he'd had to attend after Operation Grandiose. He hadn't wanted to talk about his feelings then. He didn't want to talk about them now either.

But facts he could share all the time. Facts could be absent of emotion.

They had time to kill while the investigation into the bomb at the Blackout campus took place, so they might as well talk. Besides, he was curious to learn more about this woman.

However, as full of admiration as Sami sounded about his family, she shouldn't be. He and his father had a strained relationship to this day, and his childhood hadn't been easy. All he'd wanted to do was play football, but his father had encouraged him to turn down a scholarship and to join the military instead.

He'd been so desperate to please his dad that he'd done just that.

"So you're from Alabama?" As she asked the question, her gaze scanned the crowd in the distance as if looking for any strangers lurking in the shadows. After a quick perusal, she turned her gaze back to him. "Do I remember that correctly?"

Beckett was surprised Sami recalled that fact. She'd been loopy during that conversation as fever ravaged her body. "That's right. Roll tide!"

She lifted her sandwich and pulled the two halves apart, staring at the gooey cheese as it stretched across her plate. "Nice place. Full of hometown values."

"I liked it there." He took a bite of his burger. He

was hungrier than he'd realized, and some red meat was the perfect remedy. Plus, eating was a good distraction from the otherwise heavy topics and situations they'd been dealing with.

"How long have you been out of the military?"

"A couple of years. I had the option to get out, and I struggled to know what to do. But here I am."

"Well, you're still doing good things for your country. Just in a different capacity, right?"

Beckett wished his family felt that way. But they were military for life. They didn't get out until they had to get out. Even then, they usually took a civilian job in the government.

But the longer Beckett stayed in the military, the more he'd felt himself becoming the spitting image of his father—and he couldn't let that happen. Especially not considering all the mistakes his father had made.

"I'm glad you see it that way because not everybody does," he said. "A lot of people think if you take a private security job that you're selling out. They don't realize that Blackout isn't your typical security company. Sure, we make decent money. But none of us are getting rich. We're doing this job because it still gives us the chance to help people."

"I personally feel like it's more important to do a

job you love than to chase money. But a lot of people don't see life that way. Money is the epitome of success and happiness for them."

He let out a grunt. Sami's statement surprised him. He'd assumed she was the type to love material things—that she was everything his family wasn't. He'd come from humble beginnings, and he appreciated people who worked for what they had.

Beckett wiped his mouth before turning the tables on her. "What about you? How did you become a psychologist?"

Sami's smile faded. "I don't want to overshare, but since you asked . . . my mom actually abandoned Dad and me when I was twelve. Everything seemed fine one minute. Then the next thing I knew she packed up her bags, gave me a kiss, and said she was leaving to start a new life. I never heard from her after that."

"Ouch. That couldn't have been easy."

Sami tilted her head as if trying to find the right words. "It wasn't. I mean, I had my father still, who was great. But he didn't know what it was like to be a full-time parent. His work was his life."

Beckett didn't personally want those priorities for himself. After his childhood, he knew he wanted any children he'd have to know that they came first.

<check> Always. Where they knew they were loved and accepted. Where the child wasn't caught in the crossfire of arguments between the mom and dad.

Her gaze scanned the restaurant again.

She was still on edge, wasn't she? No one could blame her after everything that had happened. There was still a madman out there who wanted to hurt her. They could pretend things were normal as much as they wanted right now as they ate, but both of them knew that wasn't the case.

"Anyway, it was on me to deal with my mother's abandonment," Sami started again. "I wanted to bounce back and move on. But when tragedy strikes, it leaves a psychological scar. It's really important that people learn to deal with those wounds in their lives. I know I had to learn how to do that."

"I can imagine."

"I suppose that's why I decided to study psychology. I knew how much therapy helped me. In so many cases today, counseling has a bad stigma, and I hate that. I want people to know that it's okay to say they need help. It's okay if they have an emotional wound. Even things we can't see with our eyes still need to be treated—just like a physical injury needs to be cared for."

"It sounds like you have very fulfilling work."

She daintily placed another chip in her mouth, chewed, and swallowed before answering. "It's hard work. You hear about some of the worst situations you can imagine. Sometimes, it seems like everything you say to your clients goes in one ear and out the other. Then you have other cases where you see honest changes in a person. You know you're really helping people move beyond their hurt. That's why I do what I do."

A surge of admiration swelled in Beckett. What was there not to respect about that statement? Sami was acting as a positive change in the world. Society needed that today more than ever.

"I think that's great." His voice sounded huskier than he'd intended. Sami had moved him more than he realized.

He could have used someone like Sami in his life as a teen when his parents had split. Not that he would have willingly opened up to a therapist. But if he'd allowed himself to do so then, Beckett wondered how different he might be now.

His dad had taught him not to ever show emotions—not to ever even smile, for that matter. Men should be tough, his father had said. Emotions weren't something to be embraced.

His mom, on the other hand, had been the opposite. She'd been all emotion.

His parents' conflicting personalities was one of the reasons they'd ended up divorced.

Sami shrugged in a down-to-earth manner that still surprised him. His first impression about the woman had been so wrong. How many times would he remind himself of that fact?

"I think it sounds like we're both trying to make a difference, just in different ways," she said. "Isn't it amazing how we need all kinds of people in this world just to make it work the way it's supposed to?"

"You're a breath of fresh air, Sami."

She shrugged, her eyes widening with what appeared to be delight before immediately sobering. "I don't know about that. But I've come a long way. I want other people to know that they can come a long way too."

Did she mean that? Did her words apply to Beckett? Could he take the pain in his own life and turn it around?

Because, in his line of work, opening up about emotional wounds wasn't something that happened. Sure, the military ordered psychological evaluations after traumatic events. But it wasn't something that any warrior ever wanted to do.

Beckett tried to keep his thoughts from going to those places right now.

Instead, he picked up his fork, ready to try the fennel citrus salad that had come with his meal. As he did, his hand suddenly went numb, and his fork clattered onto the table.

He rubbed his fingers, waiting for the feeling to pass.

"What's wrong?" Concern stretched through her eyes.

"Nothing." He grimaced. "Sometimes, my hand stops working for me."

Sami narrowed her gaze. "How long has that been happening?"

He shrugged. "Long enough. Doctors think it could be an autoimmune disorder. Either way, it doesn't bode well for a sharpshooter to have his hands go numb."

"No, I don't suppose it does."

Thankfully, his phone rang before he had to talk about this anymore.

It was Colton.

The campus had been cleared, and they were allowed to go back.

Just in the nick of time.

Because Beckett felt like he could sit here and listen to Sami all day.

He hadn't felt like that in a long time, and he didn't like the feeling.

Sami Reynolds was not the type of woman he needed to be interested in—for both of their sakes.

CHAPTER ELEVEN

BECKETT WALKED Sami up to Elise and Colton's apartment so the two of them could catch up.

As soon as Sami saw Elise, she pulled her friend into a hug. "I'm so glad you're okay."

"I'm so glad you're okay also." Elise rubbed her swollen abdomen and frowned. "That was pretty scary."

"To say the least."

Elise's gaze flickered back to Beckett as he lingered in the doorway. "Thanks for taking care of my friend."

"It was no problem." He offered a solemn nod before turning back to Sami. "Listen, I have to go do patrol duty outside. But I need to know you'll be safe. Do you plan on staying here with Elise?"

"I do," Sami said. "I've had enough excitement for the day."

"I can show her around again, just in case she forgot anything from when she came before." Elise pushed a piece of her short, dark hair behind her ear. "I'll give her a tour, show her to her room, but I promise we won't leave this building. Deal?"

Beckett nodded again. "That sounds good. I'll check in later."

Sami halfway wanted to argue and tell him he didn't need to. But she figured that would be pointless. "I look forward to it."

As soon as Beckett left and Sami closed the door, she turned toward Elise and let out a breath. Something about being with Beckett got her adrenaline pumping. She could use a little time to decompress.

"You look forward to it?" Elise raised her eyebrows as she plucked a used water glass from the table and took it into the kitchen.

Sami shrugged. "I just wanted to see how Beckett would react if I said that. He gets that little smirk in his eyes sometimes."

Elise and Sami walked toward the couch and sat down to catch up.

"Beckett is an interesting guy," Elise started.

Sami pulled a pillow in her lap before crossing her legs and turning toward her friend. "Is he?"

"The guys like to call him No-Smile Beckett."

"So I've heard. Let me guess, that's because . . . he never smiles?"

Elise snapped her fingers and pointed at Sami. "You didn't get your doctorate for no reason."

Sami shrugged. "What can I say? My powers of deduction are pretty amazing."

They both chuckled.

But Sami wasn't done with the subject yet. She had more information she wanted to find out. "Tell me more about Beckett."

Elise pressed her lips together in thought before answering. "He's a tough nut to crack. It's hard to get a good read on him. But Colton says he's a standup guy. He's the person you want on your side if trouble comes. He's faithful. Dependable. Capable."

"Single?" Sami knew she shouldn't ask the question, but she asked anyway.

"And single." Elise shot Sami a knowing grin.

"Has he ever been married?"

Most men his age had been married at least once, and Sami knew a lot of Navy SEALs' marriages ended in divorce.

"Never been married," Elise said. "Not as far as I know, at least."

Sami leaned back. "Surprising. Why has a guy like that never been married? He's good looking, he has a job, he—"

Elise shook her head and held up a finger. "I know what you're doing, Sami. You're psychoanalyzing him right now."

"You know there's nothing I like more than cracking those tough nuts."

"Oh, girl . . . you're going to be in trouble." Elise tilted her head and gave her a knowing look.

"The man saved my life. Is it strange that I'm a little curious about him?"

"Not at all."

"I mean, what events from his past have led him to this point? Is he afraid of commitment? Has his heart been broken beyond the point of repair? Has—"

"Maybe he just hasn't met the right one." Elise cast another knowing look.

"Maybe." Sami shrugged.

"I ran into him at the grocery store the first week he was here on the island," Elise continued. "As soon as I saw him step in to help an elderly woman load her bags into the trunk of her car, I knew he was a standup guy."

"Good to know."

Elise slowly released the air from her lungs as her expression sobered. "But, right now, we have other things to talk about."

Sami leaned back and let out her own sigh before nodding. Her friend was right.

This wasn't a game where her biggest concern was figuring out a person's psychological makeup. There was a lot more at stake.

Things like how to keep the people around her safe as a madman toyed with her life.

BECKETT PATROLLED THE BLACKOUT GROUNDS.

Each team member was taking turns doing duty.

After numerous incidents, they'd had no choice but to go the extra mile. Though the facility was secure with the fence surrounding it and a security guard at the entrance during business hours, they couldn't take any chances. That bomb was proof enough they needed to be extra diligent.

Back inside, the rest of the guys were researching the names Sami had given them. They needed to check alibis and look into these people's backgrounds.

In truth, Beckett preferred to be out in the field rather than behind a computer. He was a tactical kind of guy. The thought of sitting behind a desk all day had absolutely no appeal to him.

He paced the fence as his thoughts churned.

The whole Blackout headquarters was still buzzing about what happened earlier. The police were examining the remains of the bomb for any indication as to who had made it, and they were still trying to figure out how that bomb had gotten on campus.

The security footage revealed nothing. No one had sneaked onto the campus. No deliveries had been made. Nothing.

It was almost like the bomb had appeared out of thin air. But that would have been impossible. He knew his guys would find answers. They always did. However, in this case, they had no time to waste.

He scanned the woods on the other side of the fence but saw nothing. The area had been designated wetlands so it shouldn't ever be built on. That was good for them. It would give this facility more privacy.

Beckett had never seen himself as an island type of guy, but he had to admit that he loved it here. In fact, he could see himself staying for a long time.

Something about this place beckoned him to relax.

It was one more reason he'd gotten out of the military when he had. He didn't want to see himself becoming who his father was.

It wasn't that his father was a bad guy. But everything with his dad was regimented, unemotional, and routine. There was no joy in life. Instead, it seemed to be a process of following orders.

After what Beckett had experienced growing up, he wanted the important things in his life to have purpose. He'd vowed to only say I love you to one woman, and that he would only smile when he meant it—although that goal had become a running joke on his team.

The other guys took bets on when Beckett would smile next. He liked to keep them on their toes.

He looked up as he saw Colton striding toward him. "How's it going?"

Beckett nodded. "Quiet."

"That's what we like."

"Anything new?" They fell in step beside each other.

"Unfortunately, no. I just needed to clear my head for a little while so I decided to get some fresh air."

"I get that."

They walked silently for a few minutes until Colton said, "So Sami is a pretty interesting woman, isn't she?"

That was the last subject Beckett had expected Colton to bring up.

Beckett straightened, wondering exactly where his leader was going with this. "She definitely seems interesting. Very engaging. With a personality like hers, I can see why she's good at her job. She makes it easy for people to open up."

"Does that mean you opened up to her?" Colton stole a glance at him.

"Me?" Beckett pointed at himself. "When have you ever known me to open up?"

"Only on a very rare occasion. Usually around a bonfire as we're kicking back after a successful mission. But maybe it would be good for you to find someone you could talk to."

Beckett sighed, knowing exactly where this conversation was going. "I know that all you guys are as happy as clams now that you've found your dream women. But that kind of life isn't for me."

Beckett's parents had divorced when he was ten. He'd seen them fight. Heard the barbs they'd exchanged. Remembered how they had involved everybody around them in their drama and ended up splitting relationships apart because of their own complexes.

He never wanted to put himself in that position. He'd rather stay single than risk going through that kind of pain again.

It was why he rarely dated. On occasion, if somebody caught his eye, he had gone out on a few dates.

Then it always seemed like memories of his parents' divorce flooded his mind again and made him remember why being single was really the easiest way to live. He'd never met anyone that made him think the risk was worth it.

His thoughts halted when he heard a stick snap in the distance.

"Did you hear that?" he muttered.

Colton was already reaching for his gun. "I did."

They stepped away from the fence, still scanning everything for a sign of what they'd heard. It could be as simple as a wild animal.

Or it could be as complicated as a killer.

As soon as the thought went through Beckett's head, something zinged past him.

He darted out of the way before turning to see what that had been.

Not a bullet.

He would have heard a gunshot.

His breath caught when he saw an arrow protruding from the tree behind him.

"Get down!" he told Colton.

And not a moment too soon because another arrow sliced through the air.

CHAPTER TWELVE

ELISE HAD GIVEN Sami a tour of the facilities, just as promised, before showing Sami up to her room. While she was staying here, she'd have her own little apartment at the complex. The place was small but comfortable and ample.

As she looked out the window now, Sami wished she had a view of the water, but her place faced the front of the building.

Despite the circumstances, there was something peaceful about this island. Maybe it was the smell of saltwater that surrounded her. Maybe the scent put her at ease.

Movement on the front lawn caught her eye, and she sucked in a breath.

She knew Beckett was going to patrol the

grounds for a few hours. At least, that's what he'd said when he left her at Elise's.

But it looked like he was doing more than patrolling.

Sami watched as Beckett and Colton ducked behind some trees and drew their guns.

Concern filled her chest.

What was going on?

She reached for her phone, wondering if she should call someone. But who? She didn't have the phone numbers for any of the others.

She stepped closer to the window and scanned the woods in the background.

Her breath caught.

Was that someone crouched between the trees in the woods?

And what was that in his hands?

As soon as the questions filled her mind, she saw something fly through the air.

An arrow, she realized.

Someone was shooting arrows at Beckett and Colton.

Oh, dear God . . . protect them. Please.

She frowned, unable to look away from the scene, no matter how horrific the worst-case scenarios in her mind were.

The man she'd sensed earlier . . . was he behind this? Was his reign of terror still continuing?

Her first impulse was to rush outside and check on them, but she knew she couldn't step foot out of this building. She had promised not to. Besides, she'd be a proverbial sitting duck if she did.

Still, she couldn't do nothing.

Quickly, she called Elise and told her what was happening. Elise promised to alert the rest of the team so they could help.

As Sami continued to watch, the man disappeared from sight. He must have slithered back into the woods. Would it be too late for anyone to catch him? Would he get away again?

Her gut feeling told her yes.

But there was one thing she knew for sure. Her abductor knew she was here on Lantern Beach.

He wanted to send a message.

And he'd succeeded.

"WHAT'S OUR PLAN?" Beckett yelled as he pressed himself behind a tree.

"Stay alive," Colton held his gun close as if ready to use it.

But it was nearly impossible to see through the thick branches.

Beckett had just called in backup. The other guys should be here soon.

But no more arrows had been shot in the past few minutes. Had the marksman run out of ammo? Colton glanced at him and nodded. A moment later, Beckett turned, gun in hand.

He quickly searched the horizon for the archer. He saw nothing.

As he covered Colton, his leader ran toward the gate.

He was going to go after this guy.

Still, no more arrows flew through the air.

This guy was gone, wasn't he? He'd wanted to send a message, and then he'd fled.

Beckett hoped they'd be able to catch him, but this man had proven himself to be elusive.

Colton reached the gate and stayed close to the fence as he made his way toward the woods.

Beckett followed. He still didn't see any signs of the trespasser.

A few minutes later, Axel and Gabe appeared.

The four of them searched the woods.

But the man was gone. They would search for

footprints or any other evidence left behind. They'd examine those arrows.

Beckett only hoped this guy had messed up and left some kind of clue about his identity behind.

As he strode back toward the door to the main building, he spotted someone standing inside.

Sami.

As soon as he stepped through the door, she rushed toward him, concern across her features. "Are you okay?"

Her worry touched him. "I'm fine. How'd you know something was up?"

"I looked out the window and saw it happening."

"Everyone is okay," he assured her.

"That's good to know, at least." But the apprehension still didn't leave her gaze. She held up her phone. "I snapped a picture. It's grainy. You can't make out a lot. But I thought it couldn't hurt."

"Can I see?"

She handed her phone to him. He studied the picture. She was right. It was hard to make out much.

But maybe something in here would give them the lead they'd been looking for.

"Smart thinking, Sami," he told her. "Smart thinking."

CHAPTER THIRTEEN

SAMI HADN'T SLEPT WELL since the whole scenario began. Nightmares had plagued her.

But something about being at the Blackout facility must have brought her a small measure of comfort. At least she'd gotten a few hours of shut-eye.

As she lay in bed now, she glanced over at the time. Seven-thirty.

She was usually awake by five so she could do her morning devotions and get some exercise in.

She lived in a 1,000-square-foot townhouse near downtown Atlanta. The area was nice, clean, and well-kept, and she liked her neighbors. A friendly married couple lived on one side of her and a widow on the other. She called hello to them whenever she took her morning walks. She'd even had both neighbors over for a cookout once.

As she glanced at the clock again, Sami turned over in bed. It felt strange to sleep this late.

Working hard had been ingrained in her. Even when she tried to relax, she relaxed by working. Her dad used to call it the family curse. Sitting around and doing nothing was not her MO.

What would today hold? Would she find out any answers?

Sami knew she wouldn't have any peace in her life until she did.

Whoever had done this to her needed to be behind bars.

She wasn't sure what it would take before he gave up.

As she fluffed her pillow, her thoughts went to Beckett. She wasn't sure why thinking about the man made her feel so happy.

It wasn't that she wanted to date or felt like she needed to have a man in her life. She was thirty-two, and she'd gotten along so far without any problems. She'd dated a few men, and once she'd almost said yes when a boyfriend proposed.

But none of those guys had been right for her. It seemed all the men she'd dated had been more interested in what her father could do for them rather than in her. They wanted to climb their way up the chain. To work as law clerk and get their foot in the door through whatever means necessary.

Thank goodness, Sami had seen the writing on the wall before it had been too late. She wanted someone who cared about her not about what she could do for them. It was one of the challenges of being the daughter of a prominent judge.

Her phone buzzed, and she saw a message from Elise.

Come down and meet us for breakfast.

Breakfast—and some coffee—sounded perfect.

Sami quickly went through her routine before heading downstairs.

Once she reached the cafeteria, she immediately spotted Elise and Colton eating together with some other people.

She plastered on a smile as she hobbled across the room toward them. Her ankle didn't hurt as badly today. That was one thing she could be thankful for.

As soon as Elise spotted her, she pulled out the empty chair beside her and patted it. "I'm so glad you're awake. And you're looking more chipper today already."

"I'm already feeling a little better, despite everything."

"I'm glad to hear it. What would you like for breakfast? I'll get it for you."

Colton stood. "No, I'll get it for you."

Knowing better than to argue, Sami requested some yogurt, granola, and fruit.

As Colton walked away, Sami's eyes scanned the rest of the place.

She was looking for Beckett. Or was she *hoping* to see Beckett?

It would be best to stop thinking about the man. Yet that felt almost impossible. Something about him had captured her imagination and made her want to know more. She wanted to dive into what made him tick. Into why he never smiled.

Her breath caught when she spotted him step inside the doorway. But he wasn't looking at her.

Instead, he strode toward the table and sat at the opposite end. He called good morning to people before turning to talk to Gabe. The two struck up what looked like a deep conversation.

A touch of disappointment filled her.

Any attraction she felt was apparently one-sided.

But being disappointed was silly. It was better if she simply nipped this in the bud. She and Beckett were as far from compatible as safety was from danger.

Colton returned a few minutes later with a plate. But something about his expression had changed in the short time since he had left.

"What's going on?" Beckett asked.

"Ernie just called. When he pulled up this morning for work, he found an area rug rolled up and lying on the side of the road. He went to check it out and . . . there's a body inside."

Sami's breath caught. A dead body?

This had to be connected with what happened to her.

But the question was: Who had been killed this time?

BECKETT, Colton, and Rocco gathered inside the guard station, scrolling through security footage to see if cameras had picked up on anything that had happened outside last night.

Beckett had gotten a glimpse at the body, and he hadn't recognized the person. The man appeared to be in his early twenties and of Hispanic descent.

He watched as Colton fast-forwarded through a lot of nothing before slowing the video.

"Right there." Colton pointed to the corner of the screen.

It was hard to make out anything because of the darkness. But a man wearing all black, including a face mask, appeared.

And he looked right at the camera.

Beckett held his breath as he watched the man walk toward the screen. He clearly knew where the camera was located.

Beckett had a feeling he knew what was coming next.

Just as he suspected, the man pulled out some spray paint and covered the lens.

Everything went black.

Whoever was behind this knew exactly what he was doing. He was trying to send a message.

This little game he was playing was far from over.

CHAPTER FOURTEEN

SAMI STOOD near the window in the lobby, glancing outside at the police cars in the distance and anxiously waiting to hear what had happened.

Yet she knew what Colton had said.

A body had been found.

Another one.

She wanted to rush out there, to see it for herself. Not because she wanted to see a dead man. But because she wanted to know if she knew him. If she recognized him.

Sami wanted answers, and she'd do whatever it took to get those answers and return to her normal life.

This had already gone on far too long. Too many people had been hurt. Too many people had died.

Elise stepped beside her and stared out the front window at the scene playing out on the other side of the gate.

"Have you heard anything?" Sami asked.

Elise shook her head, her lips pulled into a tight line of worry. "No, not yet."

"I can't believe this is happening."

Elise placed a hand on Sami's shoulder. "I know. I'm so sorry. I can only imagine how frightening this is for you."

"It's not my fear that's my biggest concern. It's the fact that people are dying, and I think I'm the reason."

"You can't blame yourself."

Logically, Sami knew that. But that didn't stop the guilt from pounding inside her.

"Colton and his team are going to figure out what's going on," Elise said. "I promise."

"You have a lot of confidence in them."

Elise shrugged. "What can I say? They're the best of the best."

"Considering the situation they rescued me from, I can't argue with that." These guys put the men from those movies Sami had watched to shame. But with the way things were escalating, she only hoped no one else got hurt because of her.

POLICE CHIEF CHAMBERS and her crew had taken the body and were going to try to make an identification. No one had recognized the man yet, so Beckett didn't think he was an island native. They'd also shown Sami his picture, but she'd said he didn't look familiar.

Had the body been purposefully brought over from somewhere else and left in front of the Blackout facility to make a statement?

Based on what he'd heard the medical examiner say, the man had been dead for at least two days. Manner of death? Asphyxiation.

Beckett shook his head as he lingered near the guard station.

Sami had been abducted and left in a tower.

The second victim had been suffocated and left in a bed.

The third victim had been pushed from a tree-house and died of a head injury.

Now this man had been killed via asphyxiation, rolled in an area rug, and left in Lantern Beach.

What sense did any of that make?

This whole thing was twisted. That was for sure.

Just then, a new car pulled onto the scene.

Beckett watched as Chief Chambers strode toward it. She leaned in the window and spoke with the driver for a few minutes before heading toward Beckett.

"Someone is here to see Sami," Chief Chambers said. "Somebody named Wilson Broderick."

His back stiffened with apprehension. "I'm pretty sure Sami isn't expecting anyone."

Could this man be Sami's boyfriend? From everything Beckett had heard, the woman was single. If she'd had a boyfriend, his name would have come up in their investigation.

That made Beckett feel even more cautious right now.

"He claims he's one of Justice Reynolds' former law clerks and his current executive assistant," Chief Chambers continued.

Why would the judge send one of his employees without telling them first?

"I'll take it from here," Beckett said.

He wasn't going to mention this to Sami yet. He wanted to talk to this man first and find out more information.

Beckett didn't want to be too pushy or to insert himself where he didn't belong. Sami seemed capable of handling herself in situations like these.

That was just the kind of woman she was—the absolutely fascinating kind.

But he was determined to keep his distance. There were so many—too many—reasons why pursuing her would be a bad idea.

But why would Sami's father send anyone without letting Sami know first?

Before he went to talk to this man, Beckett quickly pulled up the man's picture on his phone. He memorized all the details he could about Wilson Broderick.

Thirty-five. Single. From the DC area originally. He now lived in Atlanta.

As Beckett strode toward the sedan, he noted that the man in the car looked like the person from the pictures. But Beckett still had a few questions for him.

"Can I help you?" Beckett's voice sounded more protective than he'd intended.

"I'm here to see Sami Reynolds."

"She's not expecting you."

The man leaned out the window, his blue Polo shirt looking freshly laundered and surprisingly not wrinkled—especially when Beckett considered the distance he must have traveled to get here.

"Her father sent me," Wilson said. "He thinks

that I may be able to help find the person who's behind what happened."

Beckett wasn't ready to accept such a simple answer. "Why didn't he call first?"

Wilson shrugged and glanced at his phone, tapping in a few things before turning back to Beckett. "Sorry. I'm still on the job, even while I'm here. Teleworking—a blessing and a curse. Anyway, you'll have to ask Justice Reynolds that question. I'm just doing what he asked me to do."

Beckett scowled. "We're going to need to search your car for any weapons."

"Do whatever you have to do," Wilson said. "I have nothing to hide."

Who said things like that?

In Beckett's experience: people who had something to hide.

Beckett stepped out of the gate so he could do just that.

But something about this man's reasons for being here didn't settle well with him.

CHAPTER FIFTEEN

SAMI STARED at Wilson as he stepped into the conference room. Beckett had updated her on the situation and stood close by as if reluctant to leave her side. She was fine with that. Now all she wanted was to find out some answers about Wilson's sudden —and unannounced—appearance.

Why would her dad send Wilson without letting her know? She'd tried to call her father so she could ask him that question, but he was in court. That meant he probably wouldn't be able to return her call until this evening.

"It's good to see you, Sami." Wilson stood as he stared at her.

The man had short blond hair, a fit build, and intelligent blue eyes. He'd graduated at the top of his class from law school and had the typical Type A personality that so many in the profession did. You had to have certain personality traits in order to succeed as a lawyer.

Not only that, but the man was driven and motivated, so much so that all he liked to talk about was his job. His passion was both inspiring and slightly off-putting.

Sami swallowed hard as she observed him. She'd actually gone on a couple of dates with Wilson, but she hadn't felt any chemistry between them. Plus, the fact that he worked for her father automatically ruled him out as someone she could have a future with. She would always question his true motives.

"I wasn't expecting you to come here." She lowered herself into a chair, her back feeling as stiff as her words.

"I know. I'm sorry to show up like this. But your father had a message he wanted me to give you. Clearly, he would have come himself, but as you know he's in court and can't be away."

"Did something else happen?" She leaned back in her chair, anticipating the worst.

As she did, Beckett stepped closer. He remained at her side, almost as if he were her personal bodyguard. She felt better when he was close.

Wilson pulled out his phone, found a picture, and showed it to her.

As the image came into view, she gasped. She recognized the door with the robin's egg blue paint and wreath with the buffalo check bow. "That's my front door."

"It is. Look on the doormat."

Sami blew up the image so she could see what she was looking at. "That looks like a . . . doll."

It wasn't a baby doll exactly. More like a fashion doll.

Wilson frowned. "It is. It's a doll with the head torn off and lying beside it."

Sami's heart pounded in her ears. "What does that mean?"

Wilson glanced at Beckett and then back at Sami as if he didn't want to answer the question.

Finally, he raised his chin and said, "The FBI is looking into the matter, but your father wanted me to tell you face-to-face."

She rolled her neck back as her thoughts raced. "Why would somebody leave a doll with the head torn off on my front doorstep? Is this person trying to send a message?"

"That's our best guess," Wilson said.

She squinted as she examined the photo more

closely. "The doll doesn't look like me. It looks like a man. With a beard."

She sucked in a breath.

It looked like Beckett.

The message had been received loud and clear: the man who'd abducted her wasn't finished yet. And anyone close to her could become a target.

THE NEXT TWO hours were spent debriefing with Wilson in the conference room. Beckett told Sami she didn't have to stay, but she'd insisted.

As Beckett and Colton talked to Wilson, the rest of the team looked into Lawrence Murdock and Clark Stephens—the two men who'd previously threatened her father over his law cases.

Unfortunately, both of them could be cleared. They had alibis for the day Sami had been abducted. Lawrence was on vacation, and Clark was visiting a friend in California.

They also looked deeper into the backgrounds of the people who'd been killed while Sami had been trapped in the turret. But they found no obvious connections between them and either Sami or her father.

Chief Chambers had taken the arrows that had been fired and was testing them for fingerprints. They appeared to be standard crossbow arrows that could be purchased online, but maybe they would lead to a clue.

Still, Beckett knew it could take time to get hits on fingerprints. They didn't have time to spare right now.

That essentially left them back at square one.

But as Beckett reviewed the case, he felt even more unsettled.

This person had abducted Sami. Put her in that castle and left her for dead. Then he'd killed two other people, leaving clues to lead them to her. The clues had been meticulous and well planned.

That wasn't to mention the bomb that had been left on the campus yesterday.

Now a doll had been left outside of Sami's apartment, a doll with the head ripped off.

And a dead man had been deposited outside the Blackout headquarters.

Someone was playing a very sick game.

A knock sounded at the door, and Gabe stuck his head inside. He was acting as a liaison between the Lantern Beach Police Department and Blackout.

"I have an update for you," he announced.

Colton directed him to go to the front of the room so the team could hear.

"It looks like the package was left via a drone," he started.

"Drone?" Beckett was certain that he hadn't heard correctly.

"That's right. We looked at the security camera footage, and even though the drone was off screen, we saw a shadow on the lawn. Thankfully, the cameras on the Daniel Oliver Building were untouched by whomever is behind this."

"It's a brilliant way to deliver something," Colton said. "This person got the bomb past the gate without anyone ever suspecting anything."

His words were true, but Beckett still felt unsettled.

"Anything else?"

"We've been working in depth to put whatever pieces of the bomb back together that we can," Gabe said. "It looks like the device was left in a tinderbox."

"A tinderbox?" Axel stared at him as if he was speaking a different language.

Gabe nodded. "That's right, you know, a box used to hold items to start fires."

"Do you think that was supposed to send some

type of message?" Sami's eyes narrowed with thought.

"It seems like everything this guy does is to send some type of message," Gabe said.

Beckett swung his gaze back to Wilson. "Does a tinderbox in any way relate back to any of Justice Reynolds' cases?"

Wilson thought about it for a moment before shaking his head. "Not that I can think of. But I'll double-check a few things just to make sure."

There was something they were missing, some type of message that this guy was trying to send.

Beckett and his team just needed to figure out what before this guy managed to kill or hurt somebody else.

CHAPTER SIXTEEN

SAMI FELT her head beginning to pound. Maybe this meeting *had* been too much for her.

It didn't help that Wilson kept sending her looks. What was that about? Was there another reason he'd come other than what he'd stated?

She glanced at the time on her phone. They'd been here for nearly four hours now.

Someone at one point had brought in lunch for them, and that had been a nice break. Still, the entire subject matter was draining—and they didn't seem any closer to getting answers now than they had been before.

"Why don't you go rest?"

She looked up at Beckett as his deep voice

rumbled through the room. He was watching her, wasn't he? He could sense her exhaustion.

Why did that realization bring her a small thrill?

"I'm okay." She sat up straighter and picked up her coffee.

"I think Wilson can probably handle anything else after this. You should lie down. It will help your recovery."

She thought about it another moment and almost refused. But she was really no good to anyone right now. She needed to recharge.

She finally nodded and stood. "You're right. I think I will go lie down."

Beckett stood as well. "I'll walk you back to your room."

She started to refuse again when she realized it would be useless.

Instead, he took her elbow and directed her to the door. She still had a slight limp as she walked beside him. Neither of them said anything until they reached the stairway.

"What do you think about this Wilson guy?" He kept his hand on her elbow as they climbed the stairs to the second floor.

"My father trusts him," she said. "That means a lot."

"Do you trust him?"

She licked her lips. How much did she say? For someone who encouraged people to open up, she wasn't great at being vulnerable herself.

"My entire life people have used me to get close to my father. Wilson did ask me out a couple of times. On our second date I realized he'd applied to work for my father and that he was using me to get a job. For that reason, I don't hold a great regard for him."

They paused in front of her door, and Beckett's gaze locked with hers. A surprising depth filled his eyes.

"I never even thought about what it might be like to be in a position like yours," he said. "Certainly, you have people pandering to you all the time."

She shrugged. "What they don't realize is that my father is an upright guy. He doesn't want anybody to pander to him. He makes his decisions based on what he feels upholds the law and what's right and wrong."

"He sounds like a great guy."

"He is. I'm really lucky to have him in my life."

He shifted as he glanced back at her door. "I hope you're able to get some rest."

Sami nodded. "Me too. I guess everything is catching up with me."

"How about if I come to get you for dinner in a few hours?"

"That sounds great. Thank you."

As she unlocked her door and slipped inside, she glanced back so she could watch Beckett's retreating figure.

Part of her couldn't wait to see him again.

And, in some ways, that scared her far more than the threat on her life.

BECKETT HAD to remind himself not to scowl at Wilson as he joined the meeting again. He didn't like the man being here. He didn't trust him.

Anyone who tried to use someone else for their own personal gain was immediately someone Beckett didn't trust.

Just as Beckett stepped into the room, Wilson's phone buzzed. The man's eyes widened when he looked at the screen, and Beckett immediately knew something was wrong.

"What's going on?" Beckett asked.

Wilson looked up at him, his gaze still startled.

"Apparently, a dog collar was just delivered to Justice Reynolds' house. His maintenance man found it."

"A dog collar?" Axel repeated. "What does that even mean?"

Wilson shook his head, looking truly dumbfounded. "I have no idea."

Colton crossed his arms as he stood at the front of the room. "That has to tie in with this case. This guy is still toying with us."

"First a doll, and now a dog collar?" Rocco glanced around the room at each team member. "Is this person's motive to hurt Sami? To hurt Justice Reynolds? Or do they just want to teach them a lesson? To play on their terror? Because whoever is behind this is all over the place."

"Based on other clues we've received, it's nearly impossible to put together a complete picture," Colton said. "The clues don't make sense. Yet I'm fairly confident that there *is* rhyme and reason to them."

Beckett had been trying to figure that out since all this started. "It makes the most sense that this ties back to the judge."

"I agree." Wilson sat up straighter and spread his hands on the table as if bracing himself for an argument. "That's why I'm here. As you can imagine,

Justice Reynolds wants resolution as soon as possible."

"It looks like the only choice we have right now is to start back at the beginning." Colton released a long breath. "We need to go back through everything that's happened with a fine-tooth comb and search for any clues concerning who owns that castle, the location, the breadcrumbs this guy left for us, etc. In the meantime, I'm going to send Benjamin to talk to people who live close to Sami. Maybe somebody saw something and will be willing to talk."

Benjamin James was one of the original Blackout members. The two others on the original Blackout team were still away on another assignment.

"This guy is closing in on us here," Beckett reminded them. "He's sent a bomb. Left a dead body. Shot at us with a bow and arrows. He's not going to stop until he gets what he wants."

Beckett's words hung in the room.

Finally, Colton nodded. "You're right. There's a time bomb ticking away. We just don't know how many minutes are left until it explodes."

Beckett didn't like the sound of that.

"What about the dead body?" Rocco asked. "Has anyone identified him?"

"Unfortunately, no," Colton said.

"How does he fit with our other victims?" Gabe asked.

Colton shrugged. "That's what we need to figure out."

Wilson still looked dumbfounded as he glanced at Colton. "Do you feel the judge is in any danger right now?"

Colton's jaw flexed at the man's question. "I wouldn't take any chances when it comes to this guy. Justice Reynolds needs to keep his security detail close, just in case."

Why did Beckett have a feeling this was just the beginning? What exactly did this guy want?

That was what they needed to figure out.

CHAPTER SEVENTEEN

SAMI WAS THRILLED when Beckett finally knocked on her door a few hours later. Though she'd tried to take a nap, she couldn't. Instead, she kept thinking about everything that had happened. Each incident began to replay in her mind.

Being by herself suddenly didn't seem like such a great idea after all.

"Are you hungry?" Beckett asked as he stood at her door.

Eating wasn't Sami's first priority right now. But getting out of this room was. "Yes, let's go eat."

"Great. Everybody else is downstairs."

She halted in her steps as she headed to the door, doubt washing through her. "Everybody?"

Beckett twisted his head. "Is that a problem?"

She nibbled on her lip a moment before sharing what she was really thinking. "Is Wilson there also?"

"He is. He's going to be staying here this evening."

Sami drew in a breath, unsure what to say. She didn't want to sound immature or petty. But the last thing she wanted right now was to be around that man.

"How about this?" Beckett narrowed his gaze, almost as if he was reading her mind. "I could grab some dinner for us, and we could eat on the patio. Just you and me."

Her heart lifted at the possibility. "You would do that?"

He shrugged as if it weren't a big deal. "Truth be told, I'm kind of needing a break from that guy too."

Sami fought a smile, grateful for Beckett's insightfulness. "I'm game if you are."

"Great. Let's grab some to-go containers on the way outside then."

As they walked down the hall together toward the cafeteria, Sami couldn't help but muse that Beckett was different than she'd thought he would be. She had worked with soldiers before. She knew most of them didn't like to talk about their feelings.

She also knew she could never be with someone

who couldn't talk about how they felt. Digging deeply into a person's emotional makeup was what she did for a living. She dug deeper so she could untangle people's pasts, tragedies, and emotions. But she had ascertained almost nothing from Beckett's background.

Still, something about Beckett fascinated her.

"Have you guys been able to make any progress on the case?" she asked.

"We're exploring every possible scenario," Beckett said. "I'd love to tell you that we have answers, but we don't. Not yet."

"I know you guys are working hard on it, and I appreciate that."

They paused in front of the cafeteria doors. "Speaking of which . . . a dog collar was delivered to your father today."

"A dog collar?"

Beckett nodded. "We don't know what it means, but we're guessing it's another cryptic clue."

She frowned. What could that even mean?

Beckett disappeared inside and returned a few minutes later with a paper bag full of food.

He led her to the other side of the building, and they stepped out a set of doors onto a small patio. A pergola stretched overhead and walls surrounded three sides, making the space secluded. The Pamlico Sound greeted them in the distance.

It was really beautiful. The three-piece patio dinette with its teal cushions and the potted plants scattered throughout the space made the area feel even more cozy.

Beckett turned toward her as they stood near the doors. "We want to find this guy just as much as you do. Believe me."

She offered a grateful smile. "It means a lot that you guys are putting so much into it. It really does."

He shrugged. "That's what we were hired to do."

Beckett's words hung in the air. Had he been trying to make a statement? To send her a reminder?

Either way, it was one Sami needed to hear. She couldn't let her emotions get the best of her now.

"Of course." These guys were just doing their job, what they were hired to do as Beckett had said. There was nothing more to it. Beckett's care and concern were just because he had a job to do.

Sami definitely needed to keep that in mind.

Keeping Beckett at arm's length was the smartest thing she could do. She'd be wise not to forget that.

BECKETT HANDED Sami a container with tonight's dinner inside.

She lifted the lid and closed her eyes as she inhaled the scent of roast beef and mashed potatoes. "This smells like the perfect comfort food."

"I was hoping you would think that." Beckett sat in the chair next to her, looking forward to chatting one-on-one with her entirely too much.

As he looked out, he saw the sun inching closer and closer to the horizon over the water in the distance. The sight was something that never got old. In fact, it often reminded Beckett of his place in the world.

He'd watched sunsets all over the world. Here in Lantern Beach. Back home in Alabama. In the Middle East. In Africa. Every time he was reminded that people everywhere collectively shared the experience, no matter what their place or circumstance in life.

"This is just beautiful," she muttered. "I'm surprised nobody else is out here."

"I like to come here sometimes when I need to be by myself. I try not to tell very many people what I'm doing."

"Well, it's gorgeous. And perfect. As long as no drones appear." She flashed a smile.

He raised his eyebrows. "Believe me, we have everybody keeping their eyes open for that right now."

"That's good news." She quickly lifted a silent prayer before grabbing a fork, stabbing a piece of meat, and gingerly taking a bite. "So, tell me, why do your friends call you No-Smile Beckett?"

He shrugged, his eyes dancing. "I have no idea."

She tilted her head and gave him a knowing look. "I mean, clearly, you have a problem with smiling."

"A problem?" He made sure to sound aghast. "I have no problem with smiling."

"Then why don't you?"

"I just need a really good reason first."

Sami raised an eyebrow, still studying him. "You've never had a good reason?"

"Of course I have. I just can't let the guys know that. I like to keep them guessing."

She let out a chuckle. "I've noticed you all seem to have great comradery. It's inspiring, really."

"I'll let the guys know. Inspiring others with our friendship is on our bucket lists."

Sami stared at him a moment as if trying to read his tone before bursting into laughter. "Listen to you, Beckett Jones. You're funny."

"Am I?"

She tilted her head again, still trying to figure this guy out. He was a mystery.

A tough nut to crack as Elise said.

And Sami had always loved a challenge. Especially a good-looking one.

"What are you thinking?" Beckett's nostrils flared as if he fought a grin.

"You don't want to know."

"I wouldn't have asked if I didn't want to know."

She put down her fork and decided to divulge her thoughts. "I'm thinking you probably grew up in a home with strict parents. Maybe you even felt the need to protect your mom or a younger sister. You learned it was better not to show emotions. That emotions made you feel weak somehow, and you hated feeling weak."

The light left his eyes.

She'd hit too close to home, hadn't she? Regret filled her.

"I'm sorry," she said. "I took it too far, didn't I?"

He shrugged. "No, you're right. I'm an only child, but I used to use my size to intercede for others. Mostly the kids who got picked on at school."

"You're a protector. That's a good thing."

His eyes examined her. "Do you always try to read people?"

Sami paused with her fork in front of her lips. "It's kind of my job."

He shifted, turning to fully face her. "How about you, Sami? Does anyone ever hold up a mirror to your past and show you things you didn't realize?"

His question caught her off guard, and she blinked. "I don't suppose they do. I'm so used to listening to other people and helping them that I don't really think much about my own past."

A footstep sounded in the distance, drawing them out of their conversation.

Beckett rose to his feet and withdrew his gun.

Someone was here, trying to hide their presence.

Could the killer have somehow managed to get on campus?

CHAPTER EIGHTEEN

SAMI FELT Beckett bristle beside her and knew something was wrong. As he drew his gun, her feeling was confirmed. What had he heard that she hadn't?

"I know you're there." Beckett's voice sounded like a deep growl. "Come out."

Sami pushed herself back farther into the chair, not sure what to expect.

Was this how she'd been abducted so easily? She liked to think of herself as observant about what happened around her. But maybe she should revisit that.

A moment later, someone stepped from the shadows with his hands in the air.

Wilson.

"I didn't mean to scare anybody," he rushed.

Sami released her breath, her relief turning to annoyance. "What are you doing out here?"

"I was trying to find you so we could catch up for a few minutes." He shrugged sheepishly. "I didn't mean to interrupt anything."

"You didn't interrupt anything." Sami put her fork on the table in front of her, her appetite gone. "What did you want to talk to me about?"

His gaze went to Beckett as if he didn't want to say anything in front of the man and then fluttered back to meet Sami's. "I just wanted to see how you were doing."

Why was he suddenly concerned about her? Because it would look good to her father? That was her best guess.

"I'm doing about as well as can be expected," she finally answered.

"That's good. You have a lot of people who have been worried about you."

"I appreciate the concern, but I'm being well taken care of here."

"I'm glad to hear that." He stuffed his hands back into the pockets of his khaki pants as an awkward moment stretched between them. Finally, he said,

"I'll let the two of you eat. Maybe we could catch up for a few minutes tomorrow."

"Maybe." Sami didn't want to commit to anything.

Sami and Beckett both watched as Wilson stepped back inside and away from them. Only when he was out of sight did Beckett put his gun away, sit back down, and let his shoulders relax.

"If he'd been a snake, he would have bitten me," Sami muttered, mentally berating herself for not being more on guard.

Safety is an illusion.

She wasn't sure where that thought had come from, but it seemed appropriate for a time like this.

"The question is, is he a snake?" Beckett asked.

Sami twisted her neck as she turned toward Beckett. After a moment of thought, she shook her head. "Maybe he's not the most upstanding guy when it comes to relationships. But I don't think he's a killer either." She froze as she said the words and studied Beckett's face. "Wait, you're wondering if *Wilson* might be behind this?"

"I wouldn't put anything past anyone at this point."

She shivered as she leaned back in her chair. "I don't like the thought of that."

"You're not supposed to like the thought of that."

She took another bite of her food and slowly chewed it.

As she glanced in the distance, the sun was only a half-circle on the horizon. In a couple more minutes it would be completely gone. But in the process of disappearing, it left behind a smear of beautiful colors.

"Have you ever been married, Sami?"

Her eyebrows shot up. She hadn't expected to hear such a personal question. But she didn't mind answering.

She shook her head. "Nope, never. Almost all my friends are married at this point, but I'm still single. I'm not complaining, however. Better to be single than to marry the wrong person. You?"

"No, I've never been married either. And I totally agree with your assessment."

She absorbed his words and nodded slowly.

Beckett twisted his neck as he observed her. "What are you thinking?"

She hesitated, wondering if she should share her thoughts or not. Then she decided she should dive in. "I know that most Navy SEAL marriages end in divorce. Yet here you are, and you've avoided marriage altogether."

"And you're trying to analyze why that is?" A slight smirk filled his gaze.

She shrugged. "You've just got me curious."

"Have I, Sami?" He raised his eyebrows as if humored by her statement.

She liked the easy banter they had between them.

Maybe she liked it a little too much.

Safety is an illusion.

Even when it came to flirting, she reminded herself. Even when it came to flirting.

BECKETT HAD ENJOYED TALKING to Sami. Long after the sunset, the two of them had sat on the patio and talked about life. Their childhood. What they like to eat.

Sami wasn't like Beckett thought she would be, and he was pleasantly surprised at that realization.

But, still, he also sensed something guarded about her. Did that trait come with her career? Did she feel like she needed to be strong in order to help others?

He didn't know. But, despite the caution he felt, he hoped he might find out.

He collected their dinner plates and placed them back in the containers he had brought them out in. Then he nodded toward the door, surprisingly disappointed that their time together was over.

"We should probably get inside," he murmured.

"Probably. But this was nice. Thank you for suggesting that we come out here and get away from everybody else for a bit."

"I enjoyed it also."

He waited for her to step in front of him and then placed a hand on her back.

Beckett did that a lot for Sami. Did he do that with every woman he helped?

He didn't think so.

Then again, he had asked to be in charge of protecting Sami.

It wasn't that he was showing her any favoritism. He was just doing his job.

Just doing his job.

When he'd said that earlier, he saw something change on Sami's face. Was she disappointed by those words? Did she hope that there was more to what was between them?

He couldn't let himself read too much into this.

Before long, Sami would be safe. When that

happened, she'd return to her old life, several hours away in Atlanta.

One of the things Beckett liked about this job with Blackout was the opportunity to travel. He wouldn't be chained down to one place.

But that also meant that he wasn't in the position to date anybody.

He'd be smart to keep that in mind.

CHAPTER NINETEEN

BACK INSIDE, Sami paused in the lobby.

Beckett hesitated a moment before nodding toward the hallway leading to the offices. "Colton wants to meet with the team just for a few minutes before we turn in for the night. I can walk you up to your room first."

Sami stared at the fireplace in front of her. "If it's okay, I'd like to sit out here for a few minutes."

"And then you're going to go straight up to your room?"

She had to smile. "Yes, I'll go right up to my room like a good girl."

He stared at her another moment as if trying to figure out if that option would keep her safe. Finally, he nodded—although he still looked hesitant. "Okay then. Let me give you my phone number, just in case you need it."

She pulled out her cell and added him to her contacts. Then they said good night.

Sami watched Beckett walk away, forcing herself to draw her gaze away from his broad shoulders. She couldn't remember the last time she'd felt this attracted to someone—and that realization scared her.

Could there be any worse time to feel attracted to someone?

When Beckett was out of sight, Sami walked to the fireplace and curled up in the chair closest to it.

Even though it was warm outside, there was something about a fireplace Sami always found comforting.

She stared into the flames now, mesmerized by the way they flitted in the air. After a few minutes of staring at the blaze, she let her thoughts wander to the future.

If she stayed here much longer, she would need to call her practice back and reschedule more appointments. She hated to do that.

She knew that her clients needed her. Some needed her more than once a week because the problems they were working through were that serious. But she also knew she had colleagues who could help fill the space when she couldn't be there.

Despite that, a measure of guilt hit her. She would hate to have any of her clients relapse because she wasn't there.

Since Sami taught the importance of self-care, she knew how important that was for her right now also. Every time she allowed her mind to wander, it went back to what had happened to her. There was no way in good conscience she could have a session with somebody when she knew her mind wouldn't be totally in it.

As she stared at the fire, a sound caught her ear and she stiffened.

Was she hearing things again?

She didn't think she was.

She rose and paced through the lobby toward the front door. Was that where the noise had come from?

She paused there and crossed her arms as she stared outside and waited to hear the sound again.

After several moments, she heard nothing. Maybe she had imagined it all.

Just as she started to step away, the cry came again.

Yes, that had definitely sounded like a cry.

She held her breath, waiting to hear more.

Another cry sounded followed by what was clearly a "Help me!"

Even worse, the words sounded like they'd come from a child.

Her thoughts immediately went to the little girl she'd seen playing in the lobby earlier today. She thought her name was Ada. Her dad worked for Blackout, according to Beckett.

Had the little girl wandered outside?

Was she hurt?

Either way, it definitely sounded like someone needed help.

She glanced back at the hallway where Beckett had disappeared.

Did she have time to run back and get him so he could help?

Every second counted right now.

Sami only had a heartbeat to make the choice.

AS SAMI HEARD the cry again, she knew she couldn't waste any more time.

A child needed her help.

She pushed through the door and burst outside.

Darkness surrounded her, causing a shiver to go down her spine.

She ignored it.

Instead, she waited to hear the cry again so she could know which direction to run.

As she waited, she pulled out her phone.

She started to dial Beckett's number when the cry came again.

It sounded like it came from near the gate by the entrance.

She took off in a run toward it.

As she did, she hit Send and the phone rang.

Beckett answered a moment later, a touch of worry in his voice. "Is everything okay?"

"I heard a child crying for help outside."

"Tell me you didn't go check it out by yourself . . ."

"I'm out here now, but I'm calling you." She braced herself for the lecture she knew would come.

"Sami . . ." he muttered. "I'll be right there."

She shoved the phone back into her pocket and paused near the gate.

The cry had come from the other side.

The security guard had already left for the evening and wasn't there to control the gate. Instead,

Sami pressed the after-hours button, and the opening slowly swung out.

As it did, she darted onto the street on the other side. "Where are you?"

Silence answered her.

This was definitely where the cry had come from. So where had the child gone? Sami didn't see any vehicles.

As the questions paraded through her head, a new sound filled the air.

Her heart pounded in her ears as she sensed that something wasn't right.

She heard the gate behind her click back into place, locking her out.

The next instant, three Doberman pinchers charged from the darkness toward her.

Based on the way they bared their teeth, they were ready to attack.

CHAPTER TWENTY

BECKETT SUCKED in a breath when he saw the scene playing out in the distance.

Sami stood frozen outside of the gate.

And three snarling dogs charged toward her.

He didn't have time to think about the logic of the situation. He only had time to act.

Colton and Rocco were on his heels as they ran toward the gate.

He saw Sami as she sprinted toward the gate. She shook the fence there.

But the gate was designed to close and lock automatically.

She had no way to open the gate from the outside.

They needed to reach the release button and open the gate for her.

And they only had seconds to do that before the dogs would be on her.

Colton ran toward the opposite side of the fence, clearly trying to distract the canines. "Hey, puppies! This way!"

The tactic was worth a shot.

Beckett finally reached the button and threw his weight on it.

Slowly, the gate began to open.

As it did, Sami darted inside and tried to push it closed behind her.

But before she could, one of the dogs dashed inside.

———

SAMI MADE the mistake of glancing behind her.

One of the dogs had managed to get in before the gate closed. It was now only six feet behind her and closing in quickly. Foam came from his mouth, and his eyes were lit red.

"Run!" she yelled to Beckett.

He waited for her to get close enough to take his

hand. As her fingers slipped into his, Beckett pulled her faster than she thought possible.

Without looking, Sami sensed that the dog was close. Nipping on their heels, as the saying went.

Adrenaline surged through her as she ran faster than she'd ever run in her life.

Finally, they reached the door. Beckett flung it open and pushed her inside.

Before he could dive inside himself, the dog caught his shoe, its teeth digging into it.

Beckett shoved the door shut—no doubt so the dog couldn't get inside to Sami.

As helplessness filled her, Sami pressed her hands against the glass.

Please, Lord . . . help him!

CHAPTER TWENTY-ONE

BECKETT DROPPED to his knees as he felt the dog's teeth dig into his boot. Thankfully, he still had his work boots on and the soles were thick.

But he knew that he was on borrowed time.

He turned onto his back and kicked the dog's chest.

The canine backed off.

The Doberman stood only a foot away, but it let out a low growl as he stared at Beckett with challenge in his gaze.

Beckett was going to have to think quickly.

He didn't want it to end up as a choice between his life and the dog's.

The last thing he wanted was to harm the

animal. But someone had obviously set the animal loose for the purpose of hurting someone.

The dog was clearly highly trained.

And triggered.

This situation was precarious at best.

He had to figure a way out of this.

"Hey, puppy." Beckett kept his voice nonthreatening.

The dog growled again, and more foam came from his mouth.

"It's okay, puppy." He didn't really think this would work, but maybe another great idea would hit him in the meantime.

Just as that thought went through his head, the dog lunged toward him. Beckett raised his feet again, and the dog's mouth caught his foot. The canine swung his head back and forth, viciously attacking his boot.

Again, Beckett pulled his other leg back and kicked the dog in the chest. The action pushed the dog away for a moment.

At least, Sami was safe. He found some comfort in knowing that.

But this was far from over.

The dog lunged at him again.

As his teeth sank into Beckett's boot, Beckett

braced himself to feel the dog's fangs dig into his skin as well.

SAMI BANGED ON THE GLASS, desperate to distract the dog.

She wanted to open the door and get Beckett inside, out of harm's way.

But she knew if the Doberman got into this building, more people might be hurt. She couldn't let that happen either.

Yet she hated feeling helpless. Hated watching the dog come after Beckett. There had to be something she could do.

The dog looked vicious as he swung his head back and forth, Beckett's foot clutched in his jaw.

Who had released those dogs? And why?

Just as the dog grabbed Beckett's leg, a new figure appeared.

She gasped when Gabe came into view. Where had he come from?

He shouldn't be out there. He was going to get himself killed.

What was Gabe doing? Had he lost his mind?

The dog seemed to see him at the same time Sami did, and he raised his head.

Drool dripped from the dog's mouth as he growled.

Gabe held out something.

Was that a . . . steak?

"Look what I have," Gabe called.

The dog lifted his nose into the air and sniffed.

As he did, Beckett scooted back ever so slightly.

"This is all yours," Gabe continued.

The dog continued to stare, totally distracted by the piece of meat in front of him.

Gabe held it closer.

Sami hoped the man knew what he was doing. Because if not . . . this bad situation was going to turn even worse.

"This is all yours," Gabe repeated, keeping his voice soft and light.

The next instant, he tossed the steak across the lawn.

The dog darted after it.

As soon as he did, Sami opened the door and grabbed Beckett. She pulled him inside. As she did, Gabe ran in behind them and helped Sami jerk the door closed.

"Where are Colton and Rocco?" Sami rushed as she slipped an arm around Beckett.

She couldn't help but note how he winced with pain.

"They're in the guard shack," Gabe said. "But they're safe."

Relief filled her.

She could be thankful for that, at least.

But based on the look on Beckett's face, this event hadn't been without casualties.

CHAPTER TWENTY-TWO

AN HOUR LATER, animal control had come. The dogs had been sedated and captured. Now they would begin the process of trying to figure out who the animals belonged to.

Clearly, somebody had let those dogs loose with the intention of hurting someone.

The fact that it had almost been Sami was probably a bonus to the person behind this.

"So tell us what happened again." Beckett leaned forward as they sat in the lobby. Rocco and Gabe were also present.

Sami shifted in her seat, still looking shaken. She'd already told them the story once, but he wanted to hear it again.

"I heard a little girl crying for help," she started. "I couldn't just leave her out there."

Beckett frowned. Whoever was behind this knew that a child crying for help would prey on the instincts of anyone who heard. But Sami especially. Given her background in psychology, there would be no way she could simply stay in place if a child was hurt or scared.

"I know I promised you I was going to stay inside, but when I heard how scared the girl sounded . . ." She licked her lips and stared at the fire, almost as if her mind was in another place.

"I understand," he said. "But I'm glad you called me when you did."

That whole situation could have turned out much worse otherwise.

Beckett reached down and rubbed the bandage on his leg. Thankfully, the bite hadn't been deep. But he'd most definitely felt the dog's teeth puncturing his skin.

Doc Clemson, one of the island's physicians, had stopped by and given Beckett the shots he needed, just in case the dog had any diseases.

"Nobody found a girl out there?" Sami wrapped her arms across her chest as she glanced up at him, waiting for additional confirmation.

Beckett shook his head. "There was no one."

Just then, Axel stepped into the lobby with something in his hands. "Look what I just found."

He held up the device, which almost looked like a handheld radio. He pushed a button and the sound of a child crying for help filled the air.

Sami let out a long breath before shaking her head. "Do you think that this person actually recorded a child that needed help?"

"That recording sounds too clear," Beckett said. "Too purposeful. Whoever is behind this found that recording and used it. But from a distance, it would have been hard to tell."

Sami nodded somberly. "The guy who did this . . . his modus operandi makes no sense. He abducts me, and he could have killed me, but he didn't. Then he murders two other people. Then he drops a bomb. He leaves another body rolled up in a rug nearby. And now he sends dogs out."

Beckett studied her face, trying to read between the lines. "You think this is the same person doing all this?"

"I do. It's the only thing that makes sense." She sat up straighter. "And this guy hinted that this would happen. He sent my father that dog collar."

Beckett let out a puff of air as realization hit him.

She was right. This guy had sent that clue. They just hadn't put it together yet.

Sami shook her head. "But I've spent my whole life trying to understand the way people think and operate. This person doesn't make any sense. I can't find any pattern that points to his thought process, and it's bugging me."

"When a person doesn't make any sense, what does that mean?" Rocco asked.

"In my opinion? It means they're unstable. Unbalanced."

Rocco nodded in agreement. "We need to double-check the alibis of the people involved with this again. Whoever is behind this is close. If the people on our list of suspects haven't been near Lantern Beach, then there's no way they're responsible."

"Unless they're working with somebody." Beckett's words stretched through the room.

Rocco frowned. "Unless they're working with somebody."

AFTER THEIR MEETING, Beckett insisted on walking Sami up to her room. She knew there was no getting out of it after what happened earlier. She'd broken her promise to stay inside and, as a result, Beckett had been hurt. That was on her, and she couldn't forget that fact.

As they climbed the stairs to the second floor, Sami saw Beckett reach for his shoulder and wince.

"Are you hurt?" she asked.

"I'm sure it's nothing," he muttered.

As they stopped on the landing, she paused. "It's not nothing if it's bothering you. Let me take a look."

He looked like he wanted to argue, but he didn't. Instead, he tugged off the zip-up sweatshirt he'd slipped over his shoulders earlier. Though it was summer, the breeze had turned cool.

Sami gently pulled down his collar to see the back of his shoulder. A large gash stretched there.

Sami frowned as she examined it. "When did this happen?"

"I hit something when I pushed you inside the building."

The cut was deep and wide—definitely not something that should be left untreated. "You should have probably mentioned this to the doctor. You definitely need to put some ointment on that."

"It's no big deal. I'll do it when I get back to my room."

This guy was clearly stubborn. And macho.

Neither of which came as a surprise to her.

She tilted her head and gave him a mothering look as she asked, "Do you have a first aid kit?"

"There's one in my place. Why?"

"Let me help you."

He shrugged and pulled his sweatshirt back on. "You don't have to do that."

"You're not even going to be able to look into the mirror and see where this cut is. I'll help you, and then I'll leave. I promise."

"You say that like I should be afraid of being alone with you." His eyes sparkled again.

"I just want to make it clear that I'm no threat."

Something close to amusement danced in his gaze. "Noted."

A few seconds later, he nodded. "My place is right down the hall. Let's swing by for a minute."

Sami followed beside him as he walked down the hall. At his door, he punched in a code and opened it.

When she stepped inside, she scanned the place and saw it was similar to the apartment where she was staying, only larger. Sami saw Beckett flinch as he stepped toward the living room. His wounds from the Doberman were obviously still bothering him.

"Have a seat." She pointed to a chair, happy to trade places and be the one who took care of him.

"Yes, ma'am."

"Where's your first aid kit?"

"Under the bathroom sink."

She quickly disappeared and grabbed it before returning and sitting down beside him.

"Can you take your shirt off this one shoulder so I can get to your cut?" she asked.

Silently, he pulled his arm from that sleeve and pulled the shirt up to his neck.

Sami's throat felt a little drier as she stared at his muscular back.

She hadn't been prepared for that reaction, and she quickly shoved it down. This was no time to admire the man.

Instead, she grabbed some gauze and squirted some ointment on it. Gently, she pressed it into his wound. He flinched as the cream hit his cut.

She leaned closer, trying to see his expression better. As she did, she caught a whiff of his leathery aftershave. At once, she remembered the scent from when he'd held her during the tornado.

Her cheeks flushed.

She cleared her throat and scooted back, trying to get her thoughts under control. "Does this hurt?"

"I'll be fine."

"You don't like blood, do you?" That realization brought Sami a small measure of satisfaction.

"It's not my favorite."

She chuckled at the irony. "A Navy SEAL who doesn't like blood. I guess there are things that surprise you every day."

"Speaking of surprises . . . you seem like you're pretty good at this."

She found a bandage and placed it over the cut. "I used to be an EMT."

He stole a glance back at her. "What?"

"I think there's a strong connection between physical and emotional healing. If I could learn how to help people feel better physically, I thought it would give me a better understanding of how to do the same emotionally."

"I like the way you think. When did you do that?"

"When I was in college," she said. "That's how I helped pay my way through school."

"Your dad didn't pay it for you?"

"He didn't believe in handing me anything. And he still doesn't today." She chuckled. "There were times that I wished he didn't have that philosophy. But I know, in the long run, it's been good for me."

"I see." His voice sounded raspy as he said the words.

As she pressed the last of the medical tape around his bandage, she rested a hand on his shoulder and observed her handiwork. Beckett sucked in a breath and seemed to straighten at her touch.

At once, Sami felt the tension crackling between them, and she stepped back. Her throat felt tight as she murmured, "All done."

Beckett pulled his shirt back on over his arm and then rose, his figure towering above her and reminding her of just how strong and imposing he was.

"Thank you," he muttered.

Sami stood also, a surge of self-consciousness rushing through her. This space suddenly felt much smaller than it actually was. Probably because she wanted nothing more than to step closer to Beckett. To inhale the scent of his aftershave again. To feel his strong muscles beneath her fingers.

None of which would be a good idea.

"It's no problem." She nodded toward the door, trying to get her swirling thoughts under control. "I should be going. I know you have things to do."

Beckett's gaze burned into hers until finally he nodded. "Probably a good idea."

But if it was a good idea, then why did she feel so disappointed?

CHAPTER TWENTY-THREE

BECKETT WATCHED as Sami reached for the door.

He knew he should let her go.

Despite that, he called, "Wait."

Sami turned toward him, questions dancing in her gaze as one hand still extended toward the door. "Yes?"

What are you doing, Beckett? He wasn't sure where he was going with this.

He remembered their earlier conversation and how easily it had come. Thought about how worried he'd been about her when he'd seen those dogs. Reflected on how different she was than what he'd originally assumed.

"I make a mean hot chocolate," he finally said. "Would you like some?"

She narrowed her gaze. "Hot chocolate?"

He shrugged. "What can I say? It's my guilty pleasure."

She didn't say anything for a moment until finally nodding. "A warm drink sounds good."

"Great." He extended his arm behind him.

Sami entered the kitchen area and perched on one of the stools at the breakfast bar. As she did, Beckett began pulling out everything he needed. He put some milk on the stove to begin warming it.

"Impressive." Sami nodded slowly as she watched him work. "I have to admit that I halfway expected you to pull out a little packet of powdered milk and chocolate."

"Oh ye of little faith."

"You surprise me. That's a good thing."

He stole a glance up at her. "Did you think I was a stuffy old vet?"

"I don't know how I thought you were. But—" She stopped abruptly, as if she'd caught herself before saying something she would regret.

"But what?" He paused from grating a chocolate bar.

Her cheeks heated as she glanced up at him. "I don't know who I thought you were, but the person I'm discovering is quite impressive."

Her words caused his heart to skip a beat.

She sounded so sincere. And a kudo from Sami meant the world to him.

"I hold that as a high compliment," Beckett said. "Especially coming from you."

She shrugged. "I mean it. You've saved my life. Numerous times now. I can't say thank you enough. I know you're just doing your job—"

She *had* caught onto that earlier, hadn't she? When the words had left his mouth at dinner, he'd wondered if that was the impression she was left with. It hadn't been his intention.

Or had it? Had it been his way of pushing her away? Of protecting his heart?

He opened his mouth, unsure what to say.

Thankfully, he didn't have to say anything because Sami continued. "I just wanted to remind you that I wasn't the one who actually hired you."

He wasn't sure where she was going with this, but he was certainly curious. "But your dad did hire us."

"He hired you to find answers, not to protect me." Satisfaction glimmered in her gaze.

Beckett dumped the chocolate into the milk and stirred, watching it melt in the warm liquid. "That's one perspective, I suppose."

He liked that perspective. It meant that he didn't need as many professional boundaries.

Then again, maybe professional boundaries were good.

Especially when he felt as attracted to Sami as he did.

SAMI TOOK the mug of hot chocolate from Beckett and grinned. He'd even added some whipped cream and shaved chocolate on the top. It formed a Pinterest-worthy picture.

"Would you like to sit on the balcony?" Beckett nodded toward the door in the distance.

"That sounds great."

They stepped outside and sat on a loveseat glider there.

Sami tried to take a sip of her hot chocolate, but it was still too warm. Instead, she rested it on a side table.

"You have some cream on the tip of your nose." Beckett's eyes danced.

Quickly, she reached up and wiped it off with the back of her hand. "Good to know."

Beckett's gaze caught with hers. "You're really

beautiful, you know."

She felt her cheeks heat. Maybe it was because she'd expected a smart aleck comment. Instead, he'd sounded so serious. And his gaze was so warm.

Gently, he took her hand and rubbed his thumb across the back of it.

Fire spread across her skin.

Suddenly, nothing else around Sami mattered.

Or existed.

Just her and Beckett and this moment.

"Sami?" His voice sounded deep, gravelly as he leaned closer.

"Yes?"

"I know I shouldn't say this . . ."

"Say what?" She held her breath as she waited.

"I really want to kiss you right now."

"I'm not sure how I feel about kissing a man I've never even seen smile." Her throat felt dry as she said the words, and she couldn't stop staring at his lips. She wanted to kiss him also. Yet getting too close brought its own kind of fears.

Right now, she would tell her clients that they couldn't let their fears hold them back from what they really wanted—as long as what they wanted was healthy.

And that was the question. Was Sami flirting

with the idea of exploring a relationship with Beckett? And was that wise considering how different the two of them were?

"You've never seen me smile?" He lifted his eyebrows.

She swallowed hard when she saw the hypnotizing look in his gaze. "Never. I don't even know what it takes to make you smile. Is there anything?"

"There's one thing I can think of."

"What's that?" She lifted her head, curious about his answer.

"This." He leaned toward her, and his lips covered hers.

A whoosh of warmth filled her chest cavity, followed by a surge of adrenaline that made tingles dance across her skin.

Before she could overthink anything, Sami reached up and wrapped her hands around his neck. Her fingers explored his hair. His soft beard. His strong shoulders.

He pulled her closer as the kiss deepened, sweeping her into another world—one she'd be happy to never leave.

A few minutes later, they both reluctantly pulled away. As they did their gazes met.

A grin stretched across Beckett's face.

A grin.

She supposed that answered her question.

"Kisses make you smile . . ." Sami's voice sounded scratchy as the words left her throat.

"Kisses with you do."

She liked the sound of that—entirely more than she should.

CHAPTER TWENTY-FOUR

SAMI FLUNG her eyes open and sat up with a start.

Panic raced through her. Where was she?

She spotted Beckett leaning back into the cushions of the couch beside her, and she let out the air that had frozen in her lungs.

They were on the couch. In his living room.

They must have fallen asleep while watching TV together. Her head had been firmly planted on his chest.

Beckett offered a lazy smile as he stared at her. He'd obviously been awake for longer than she had. "Good morning."

She pushed a lock of hair behind her ear before running her hand over her face. She really hoped she hadn't snored. And that she didn't have the imprint of his shirt on her face.

"What time is it?" she asked.

"Seven. You were sleeping hard," Beckett muttered, warmth flooding his gaze.

"I was." She blinked a few times. "I haven't slept like that since . . ."

Beckett's hand rested on her back, silently indicating that she didn't have to finish that statement.

Since she'd been abducted.

Sami usually had too many nightmares to rest. Fear had reared its ugly head in those twilight moments before sleep came.

But last night . . . she'd slept like a baby.

Probably because Beckett had been close.

Beckett—who'd made it clear he would protect her with his life.

As she remembered their kiss, her cheeks flushed.

It had been incredible.

Unexpected.

And a bad idea.

She'd done what she vowed to never do.

She'd let her emotions get the best of her. Carry her away. Let her mind turn idealistic and believe marriage could be the happy place she'd always dreamed it would be.

Now Sami had to figure out what she was going to do about it.

She stood, feeling more self-conscious than she would like. She cleared her throat as she looked at Beckett.

But instead of speaking, her gaze went to his lips.

She'd like nothing more than to recreate that kiss from last night. To feel safe. Protected. Cared for.

She cleared her throat again, wishing it was that easy to clear her thoughts.

She couldn't let her mind go there.

Beckett seemed to sense her thoughts, and his lips tugged again as if fighting a smile.

"Now you're grinning?" She gave him a knowing look.

"You're just awfully cute when you let your guard down." He shrugged, that mischievous gleam still present.

Let her guard down? That's what she was doing, wasn't it? And Sami *never* fully let her guard down— not in her line of work.

Yet she had with Beckett. First, when he'd rescued her. Then, when they'd shared that kiss.

She pointed toward the door with her head, unable to resist the urge to flee.

"I should probably go before people ask questions," she finally said. But her issue was more the fact that she wanted some time to clear her head.

Beckett stood. "Of course. Whatever you're comfortable with."

He paused in front of her, and she started to reach for him. To rest her hand on his chest. It just felt so natural, like they'd done it a thousand times before—even if they hadn't.

Sami stopped herself just in the nick of time.

She pointed at the door again. "I'll go. And I'll see you later."

"We're having a meeting at nine. We'd love for you to join us."

She nodded. That would give her a couple of hours to clear her head so she wouldn't look like a bumbling fool with a schoolgirl crush.

"Sounds good." The words sounded more like a croak as they left her throat. "I'll see you there."

Then she fled like Joseph fleeing the temptation of Potiphar's wife.

BECKETT HAD to remind himself to stay focused.

Which was something he *never* had to do.

Focus was his middle name.

But now his thoughts seemed to swirl every time he thought about Sami.

To make matters worse, he couldn't stop thinking about her.

"How's your dog bite healing?" someone asked.

Beckett jerked his head toward his door, and he saw Colton stride into his office. Beckett had totally zoned out. Again.

"It feels fine." He rubbed his shoulder where his cut was, the one that Sami had treated and bandaged for him. "Any luck tracking down the dogs' owner?"

"The police are still looking into it. Cassidy and her crew are looking into any footage from the ferry to check for anyone coming over with three Dobermans in his or her vehicle. The whole thing is very strange."

"In all my years, I have to say I've never experienced anything like that before." Beckett felt his muscles tighten every time he remembered that dog's teeth clamping down on his foot and leg.

"I think we can all safely say that." Colton frowned. "Gabe found an area in the woods where it looked like a car was parked. Our guess is that the perpetrator stopped there, set up the recording, and then waited for someone to step outside the gate."

"The person behind this is calculated."

"Yes, he is. But no one is perfect. He's going to mess up eventually."

"Let's hope." Beckett looked at his computer again and absently tapped his fingers against the desk.

Colton paused and narrowed his eyes at him. "Is everything okay?"

Beckett nodded, maybe a little too quickly. "Of course. Why do you ask?"

"Because you seem a little . . . distracted."

Beckett shrugged again, wondering if someone had seen Sami leave his apartment this morning and had told Colton. "Maybe I just need more coffee."

Colton slowly nodded. Beckett was thankful his friend didn't press for any more details. After all, Sami was best friends with Colton's wife. If Beckett messed up and hurt Sami—which he had no intention of doing—he could be in trouble.

Mixing relationships with work was always tricky. Though Sami was correct when she'd said she wasn't a direct client, Beckett knew the lines were blurry and that he would have to be very careful.

But right now, he was simply anxious to figure out who was behind these crimes that had occurred.

"One more thing you should know," Colton said. "We have an FBI agent on his way to speak with us."

Beckett's back muscles tightened. "FBI?"

"He's working the case on Justice Reynolds, and he has some questions for Sami."

"Does she know about this yet?"

Colton shook his head. "I was going to tell her when she got down here."

Beckett nodded and wondered how she was going to handle that update.

CHAPTER TWENTY-FIVE

SAMI FELT something different in the conference room as soon as she stepped inside.

She'd been trying to calm her anxious thoughts this morning. She'd called her practice and caught up with her colleagues. She'd tried to call her dad, but he didn't answer, nor had he returned her call. She knew he was busy with this trial, but she still worried. It wasn't like him not to be in touch.

Instead of worrying, she'd spent some time in prayer.

Afterward, she'd felt more at peace.

Until her gaze went to the stranger wearing a suit sitting on the other side of the table. The man looked to be in his mid-forties with dark hair and a clean-shaven face.

Who was he? What was he doing here?

Clearly, there was something she didn't know.

"What's going on?" Her mind jumped to worst-case scenarios. Had something else happened? Was her father okay?

"This is Special Agent Mike Rogers with the FBI," Colton said. "He's working the case and trying to figure out what's going on concerning the threats against your father and the events that have happened to you. He wanted to come here himself and ask you a few questions."

Sami felt herself snap into her professional demeanor. Her shoulders stiffened. Her actions became more measured. Her words more careful. "Of course. I'll do whatever is necessary to help figure out who's behind this. But you're not the one I spoke with when I was in the hospital."

Rogers' expression remained stoic. "Special Agent Marco Sanders is still working the case. He regrets that he couldn't come himself. He's remaining in Atlanta so he can work the angles there."

"I see," Sami muttered.

Beckett rose and pulled out a chair for her. As he did, Sami willed her cheeks not to redden as she sat down beside him.

Why was she letting this man have this effect on her? Why was she letting her mind replay that kiss over and over again?

"Unfortunately, I'm here to do more than ask questions." Special Agent Rogers shifted in his seat. "I also have a couple of updates for you."

"Updates?" Tension straightened her spine. "What's going on?"

"First of all, we found fingerprints on that doll that was left outside your house."

Sami's breath caught as she realized the implications of what he was saying. "Whose were they?"

"A man named Dan Blake."

She squinted as she processed the familiar name. "My neighbor? He's a nice enough man. Married. Quiet. An engineer and avid golfer."

"He's also the one who found the doll outside your home," Rogers said.

She let out a breath. "So that makes sense then. He probably touched it."

Rogers nodded. "That's our suspicion as well, but we want to cover every angle. Have you ever had any problems with him?"

Sami shook her head. "No, never. He and his wife are respectful and keep to themselves. Maybe a little standoffish at times, but to each his and her own, right?"

The agent nodded. "I have to ask these questions, you understand."

"Of course."

"The second update that I wanted to give you is this. Your father's home was broken into last night."

Sami sucked in a breath and sat upright. "Is he okay? Was he hurt?"

From the corner of her eye, she saw Beckett start to reach for her. Then he seemed to think better of it and rested his hand back in his lap.

"Your father is fine." Rogers sounded coldly professional, so much that it was almost off-putting. "He wasn't home when it happened, and we believe that the break-in is somehow linked to this court case that's happening right now."

"I'm not sure if that makes me feel better or not." She frowned.

His gaze locked with hers. "I just wanted to let you know that we're doing everything within our power to get to the bottom of this. If it's okay, I'd like to review everything that we know about this case so far."

Sami leaned back in her chair, feeling an unseen weight press into her. "I hope you have a lot of time."

WHEN THEY BROKE for lunch a few hours later, Beckett hoped he might grab a few minutes alone with Sami.

But as soon as they stepped out into the hallway, Wilson appeared. When he spotted them, he released the handle of the rolling suitcase he pulled behind him and shifted the sports jacket he had draped from one arm to the other.

"I need to get back to Georgia," he said.

Sami nodded stiffly. "I hope the trip here was worth it."

"I'm not really sure if I was much help. But at least I'll be able to tell your father that you're doing okay."

Sami narrowed her eyes as she studied his expression. "Is that why he really sent you? Because he wanted to make sure I was okay?"

Wilson shrugged, his gaze still aloof and almost nervous. "You know your father. He likes to protect the people he loves."

"Yes, he does."

"Now that his house has been broken into, maybe I'm needed more there than here."

Beckett watched the exchange carefully. He had

a feeling there was more to this conversation than Wilson wanted to let on.

Wilson had come here because he wanted to get into Sami's good graces. He was one of *those* people. The kind that liked to suck up in order to advance themselves.

Personally, Beckett would be happy to see him gone. He'd be one less person they'd need to worry about.

Wilson grabbed the handle of his suitcase again. "I'm going to catch the ferry. I just wanted to tell you goodbye."

"Thank you. Please tell my father that I'll be home soon and that I hope this court case ends soon."

"Who knows how long the jury will deliberate once the trial itself is over? This is probably the worst time ever for something like this." Wilson offered a half eye roll.

Beckett bristled again. How could he put something like Sami's safety on a timeline, comparing it to an inconvenience? Sami's life had been threatened on more than one occasion. She was lucky to be alive.

Wilson offered a nod before turning and heading down the hallway.

As he did, Beckett turned toward Sami. She'd showered, and her hair fell down her shoulders in glossy waves. There was so much he wanted to say to her.

But something about the look in her eyes made him pause. What exactly was going through her mind right now? Something about her gaze made her seem more closed, more standoffish.

Before he had the chance to ask, Rocco strolled up beside him. "Have you talked to Ernie today? Nobody has seen him."

"No, I just assumed he was working the front gate as always."

Rocco shook his head. "He didn't show up for work."

"Are you sure he just didn't have a day off?"

"That's what I'm trying to figure out. I don't want to disturb Colton right now if I don't have to. He's talking to Special Agent Rogers. Either way, I'm going to need to head down there so I can let Wilson out."

Beckett nodded. He hoped that everything was okay. Given everything that had happened lately, there were no guarantees.

CHAPTER TWENTY-SIX

AFTER ROCCO STRODE down the hallway, Beckett turned toward Sami. "Would you like to grab some lunch together? I have a few minutes to kill while we try to get up with Ernie and see why he didn't show up today."

As Sami glanced up at him, she felt her heart jump into her throat. She wanted to say yes. She wanted to pretend like she was carefree and that she believed in happy-ever-afters. After all, wasn't that what she talked to other people about? Not being your own worst enemy?

But something inside her kept putting on the brakes. Some kind of internal nagging reminded her that the odds were stacked against her and Beckett having any kind of future together.

"I wish that I could." Her voice squeaked out, unusually high. "But I really need to get up to my room and make some more calls to my practice. I'm going to need to cancel some appointments, and I can't keep putting this off."

Beckett stared down at her, questions lingering in his gaze.

He sensed she was pulling away, didn't he?

Sami wished that she could explain. But she couldn't. Because she didn't understand her reaction herself. She still needed more time to evaluate herself, to dig deeper into her feelings.

Last night had been wonderful. There was nothing about Beckett not to like. But the fact remained that, according to the personality tests she'd taken, he wasn't her type. She didn't want to set herself up for failure.

Right now, she needed space until she could understand the very emotion she was supposed to be an expert on.

"I understand. Can I bring you something to eat?"

She shook her head. "I grabbed some breakfast on the way down, and I'm not very hungry still."

He stared at her another moment before nodding. "Okay then. We'll talk later."

"That sounds good." She offered a forced smile.

She had to admit that the confusion inside her wreaked havoc with any sense of peace she'd had earlier.

She needed to figure out how to handle this situation, how to proceed with Beckett.

Because she knew, deep down in her heart, she'd never felt this way about a man before.

And maybe that was what scared her the most.

BECKETT HAD BEEN CHARGED with tracking Ernie down. He had called the man's cell phone again, but there was no answer. The next step was to go by his house and make sure he was okay.

It wasn't like Ernie to do this. The man was in his early forties, divorced, and an island native. Colton had trained the guy himself, and Ernie had never shown any signs of incompetence.

That was what made this even more unsettling.

First, before he did anything, Beckett found Rocco in his office.

"I need to drive out to Ernie's place," Beckett said. "I don't want to leave Sami by herself, however. Would you mind just keeping an eye on things?"

"Of course. That's no problem."

Hesitation pressed on him as he left the campus.

What had changed with Sami? He sensed the shift. In his gut, he knew that something was different.

Did she regret the fact they'd kissed? She hadn't seemed to regret it at the time. In fact, she'd seemed all in—as had he.

Questions pounded through him. He didn't want to overthink this, especially when Sami's safety was his first priority.

As soon as he got a chance, he needed to pull her aside and ask her what she was thinking. There was no need to beat around the bush, as the saying went.

For now, Beckett drove out to Ernie's. As he gripped the steering wheel, his left hand went numb again.

Neuropathy was what his doctor had called it.

Ever since the team returned from a mission in Africa, they'd all suffered from various symptoms. Their commander said it was because of a substance that had been sprayed on them during the battle. Rocco had migraines. Axel's vision blurred. Beckett's hands went numb. Gabe , on occasion, had muscle weakness.

Their symptoms formed a strange picture, but

Beckett had given up trying to figure out what they'd been sprayed with. The damage was done, and doctors had said there was nothing they could do about his condition.

It was just one more reason he'd gotten out of the military when he had.

He pulled up to Ernie's place. The man lived in one of the older homes on the island, a smaller fishing cabin. It was located close to the center of the island but wooded lots stood on either side of the property.

For years, Ernie had been a commercial fisherman. But a back injury had taken him from that job. He'd worked for Blackout for eight months, and all the staff loved the man. In fact, he'd almost taken on a fatherly role for many of the people onsite.

Beckett knocked at the door, but no one answered.

However, the man's car was parked outside.

Beckett walked to the back door and knocked.

There was still no answer.

Not ready to give up, he peered in the windows. But Beckett didn't see any signs of life inside the house.

He'd check out the inside just to be certain.

Beckett twisted the door handle. It was unlocked.

"Hello? Anyone home?" Beckett stepped inside, remaining on guard.

No answer.

Carefully, he moved around the small house, checking every space.

But Ernie wasn't here.

What happened to the man?

Had he gone for a walk?

Beckett didn't know. But he had a bad feeling brewing in his gut.

When he was sure Ernie's place was clear, he started back toward his truck. To cover all his bases, he decided to check out the property before leaving.

He paused near the edge of the woods and frowned at something on the ground.

Was that . . . an inhaler?

Could this be tied with the case?

He didn't know. But he would take it back to Blackout, just to be certain.

As he reached down to pick it up, a shot rang through the air.

Beckett ducked to the ground as he realized a gunman was firing at him.

CHAPTER TWENTY-SEVEN

SAMI SPENT the next hour and a half on the phone, trying to rearrange appointments.

As much as Sami might like to stay here on Lantern Beach until she felt safe, she realized that wasn't an option. Her clients needed her, and she felt like she was letting them down by being gone for so long.

Whatever happened, her time here would have to come to an end soon. She couldn't hide out forever—despite what her father might want.

And that was another reason why she and Beckett would never work out. She would eventually return to her life. There wasn't room for another psychologist here on the island. Elise had first dibs on anything like that.

There were so, so many reasons why they would never work out.

After getting off the phone, Sami leaned back on the couch to collect her thoughts.

But every time she heard a noise, she found herself flinching. Her mind rushed back in time to when she was in that turret all alone. She remembered the despair. The isolation.

She remembered the realization that she wasn't as strong as she thought she was—or as strong as she had always thought she needed to be.

Her dad hadn't outwardly placed any pressure on her but growing up as the daughter of a prominent judge held some basic social expectations. Things like keeping her chin up. Not letting down her guard. Among other things.

Then as a psychologist, Sami had also found she needed to protect herself. While in normal relationships it was expected to give and take, to listen and to open up, it was different in a counseling relationship. While she could on occasion share something she'd overcome in her own past, it was better to keep boundaries in place.

Some people who came to her thought that Sami had all the answers. They depended on her for every bit of advice on nearly every area of their lives. She tried to teach them to make decisions on their own. But they didn't all do that.

Her thoughts wandered back to Beckett again. What was he doing? Had he found any answers?

As her phone buzzed, her breath caught.

Was she secretly hoping that Beckett was contacting her?

Instead, a message from that familiar unknown number appeared.

The words caused a shot of fear to go through her.

Are you expecting guests?

What in the world did *that* mean?

She didn't know, and part of her didn't want to find out.

———

BECKETT DUCKED INTO THE TREES, trying to spot the person shooting at him.

In the distance, he thought he saw the gleam of a gun barrel.

He tried to creep closer to that inhaler.

It was obviously important.

But as he did, a bullet hit the ground in front of him.

This guy wasn't going to let him get any closer.

Beckett drew his own weapon.

Aiming in the distance, he fired a shot.

As he did, he felt that tingling feeling in his fingers again.

Not now.

This would be the worst time for his neuropathy to kick in.

Sweat spread across his brow as he anticipated his next move.

The gunman fired back, several bullets spraying the ground around him.

Beckett needed to take cover.

And he needed to get that inhaler.

His gaze went to the device on the ground again. It was still there, halfway between Beckett and the gunman.

But there was nothing to hide behind between here and there. Just an open expanse. The other guy had a heads-up on him because of the woods where he was located.

That only left Beckett with the choice of trying to

scare the man off. Maybe this guy would run out of ammo. Then Beckett could grab the inhaler and go after this man.

Beckett shook out his hand before aiming at the shooter again.

But the tingles were still there.

Despite that, he managed to fire.

But the man ducked behind a tree just as the bullet came at him.

The man peeked out again and aimed his gun.

But this time it wasn't at Beckett.

He glanced at the ground just in time to see a bullet hit the inhaler. The device exploded into several pieces.

The gunman took off. Beckett heard him running through the woods. Then he heard a car door open.

He couldn't let this guy get away.

But as he ran back to his own vehicle, he paused.

His tires were flat.

They had been sliced.

Just as that thought went through his head, a car squealed off in the distance. He ran down the lane, trying to get a better glimpse of the vehicle.

He saw a dark sedan. But it kicked up a cloud of

dust and made it impossible for him to read the license plate.

Beckett bit back a few choice words.

He had been close. So close.

But at least he still had the pieces of that inhaler.

CHAPTER TWENTY-EIGHT

SAMI COULDN'T DECIDE who to call about that text message she'd received. Beckett seemed like the most likely choice, but part of her wanted to avoid talking to him for now.

Don't be immature, she scolded herself.

For that reason, she dialed his number anyway, but he didn't answer.

That was strange. Beckett seemed like the type who would answer, especially given the level of worry he felt about her.

Sami frowned, trying not to read too much into it.

Instead, she called Colton and relayed the message about the text to him. Thankfully, Elise had given her his number.

"Thanks for letting us know. We'll try to ping the location of the number again, but I'm not hopeful that we'll have any hits. We haven't yet."

"I understand. I just wanted to let you know."

"No problem."

"Colton?" Sami hesitated before asking her question.

"What is it?"

"Have you talked to Beckett?"

Colton hesitated a moment, just long enough for Sami to feel a surge of anxiety.

"Colton . . . what's going on?"

"Beckett went to check on Ernie. While he was there, someone shot at him."

She gasped. "Is he okay?"

"Beckett is doing fine. But he's caught up right now talking with the police. He'll be back before too long."

"I'm glad he's not hurt. If there's anything I can do, let me know."

"Will do."

As Sami ended the call, she leaned back on the couch and frowned.

Beckett had been shot at. Thankfully, he was okay. But what if that hadn't been the case? What if

Beckett ended up being the next casualty of this killer?

How would Sami ever live with herself?

"I'LL PUT out an all-points bulletin so everyone can be on the lookout," Chief Chambers said as she stood in front of Ernie's house. "We'll also start searching the island for Ernie. I don't like the sound of this."

Beckett had just finished telling Chief Chambers what had happened. He hadn't even had to call her.

A neighbor had reported the gunfire.

"This guy was right here . . ." Beckett shook his head. "I was so close to catching him."

She nodded at his tires. "He obviously had a plan."

"My best guess is that this guy dropped his inhaler when he grabbed Ernie," Beckett said. "He must have realized his DNA could be on it and came back to retrieve it."

Cassidy had already taken the pieces as evidence.

"Maybe we'll get a hit at the lab," Cassidy said. "Unfortunately, these things take time."

Beckett frowned again. "And time is something we don't have."

"I don't like what's going on here. Given everything else that's happened, I fear for Ernie."

Beckett rubbed a hand over his jaw. "Me too. One other thing is bothering me. Shooting at people doesn't appear to be this guy's MO. I think when he saw me, it threw him off guard."

"I think you're right. This guy is all over the place as far as his methods. I've never seen anything like it. At least, we have the inhaler now—even if it is in pieces. Maybe it will provide some answers." Cassidy nodded at his truck. "How about if I get Dillinger to give you a ride back?"

"That would be great. I'll have someone tow my truck so I can have the tires replaced."

For now, he got a ride back to the Blackout headquarters with Officer Dillinger.

He had a bad feeling that Ernie's disappearance might have something to do with everything else that had happened. He just wasn't sure how all the pieces fit yet.

Time was running out for them to figure out exactly what this guy was going to do next.

He had Dillinger drop him off at the gate. But he

paused before punching in his code to get inside. What was that on the ground?

It almost looked like . . . a piece of bread.

Who had left a piece of bread outside?

It seemed especially odd considering there wasn't a lake nearby where people liked to feed ducks. Nor did most of the people coming through the gate bring food with them. They either ate in the cafeteria or cooked in their apartment.

Was this in some way relevant?

Beckett started to reach for it.

Maybe he'd document it, just in case.

Given all the other strange clues they'd encountered, he couldn't rule anything out.

CHAPTER TWENTY-NINE

SAMI'S PHONE BUZZED AGAIN, and she glanced at the message there.

Look out the window.

Sami's breath caught as she stared at the words.

The text had come from the same number as the other cryptic messages.

If she walked to the window, would this man try to shoot her? Was this a trap?

She didn't know.

With a touch of hesitation, she walked toward the window on the far side of the apartment. On the other side of the fence surrounding the Blackout campus, she spotted a police car.

A police car?

She squinted. Was that Beckett standing by the gate?

She watched as the police car pulled away.

But Beckett didn't try to come inside. He paused and studied something on the ground.

A bad feeling brewed in her stomach.

What was going on here?

She glanced at her phone, but there were no other messages there.

Quickly, she dialed Beckett's number. He answered on the first ring.

"Beckett, I don't know what's going on, but I think you might be in danger," she rushed.

"What do you mean?"

"I just got a text saying I should look out the window. When I look out the window, I can see you."

She watched as Beckett glanced around.

"I don't see anything, Sami."

Panic bubbled inside her as the unknown pummeled her thoughts. "I just don't want you to get hurt."

"There's a piece of bread on the ground," he said. "That's it."

Bread? What sense did that make? "Don't touch it."

"It looks fine, Sami."

She pressed herself farther into the window, almost feeling like she was helpless and trapped in that turret again. She could hardly breathe as she watched.

"Please, Beckett . . ." she croaked.

After a moment of quiet, he finally said, "Okay, I won't do anything risky. Thanks for the heads-up."

As she ended the call, she knew for certain that she cared about Beckett entirely more than she was comfortable with.

Now she prayed that nothing happened to him.

"IT LOOKS like a piece of bread to me." Colton stared at the ground.

Beckett followed his gaze and stared at the only thing out of place in this area. "I don't see anything suspicious. There's nothing beneath the slice—not best I can tell. But Sami is concerned, so I didn't touch it."

"The text she received is suspicious." Colton frowned. "But I think this guy could be playing mind games with us now."

Beckett was inclined to agree. "One other fact

remains. If this guy told Sami to look out the window right as I pulled up, he's obviously been keeping an eye on this place. However, I can't imagine that he would have had the time to get back here. I wasn't at Ernie's very long talking to Cassidy. Besides, it would be pretty brazen to follow me here after he'd just gotten away."

"Agreed." Colton glanced around. "I'm going to call Axel and see if he'll come out here with a metal detector, just in case it's wired or something. He can check around the bread as well as the surrounding area for anything suspicious."

It all seemed like overkill, but, given the circumstances of the past several days, they needed to take every precaution possible. "Good idea."

Axel appeared a few minutes later and ran the device over the bread. Nothing beeped.

It appeared the substance was nothing more than what it appeared: bread.

As Axel scanned the rest of the area, Colton turned back to Beckett. "By the way, right before you called me to come out here, we got a hit on the dead guy found outside the facility."

Beckett straightened. "And?"

"His name was Amos Sanchez. He's from Charlotte. Twenty-five. Works construction."

"Did his family or friends say anything about him taking a trip here?"

"No, the last time he was seen was after work two days ago. He was going to get drinks with some friends, but he never made it home."

"And he died of asphyxiation?"

"That's right. Asphyxiation due to inhalation."

Beckett tried to let that sink in, but he needed more details. "You're going to have to spell that out for me."

"It appears he breathed in a large dose of helium. Lack of oxygen caused him to pass out and eventually die."

"Another odd puzzle piece."

"I can't argue with that. One other thing I learned. This guy lived in Atlanta for a while when he was thirteen."

Beckett's breath caught. That couldn't be a coincidence. "What about the other victims?"

"Here's where it gets interesting. Both of them also lived in Atlanta for a short time period . . . about ten years ago."

His pulse quickened. "That's our connection."

Colton nodded. "Exactly. Now we just have to figure out what ties all these people together."

"And potentially ties them with Sami."

Speaking of Sami, Beckett needed to give her an update.

He glanced back at the building, wondering if she was still watching this from her window. Knowing Sami, the answer was yes.

"I have a hit." Axel's voice pulled them from their conversation.

They turned toward him.

He pulled some gloves on before plucking a small black device from between some tree bark. "It's a camera. He's been watching us."

Tension pulled across Beckett's chest.

This was one sick guy they were dealing with.

He didn't even want to know what the perp was planning next.

CHAPTER THIRTY

SAMI STOOD AT THE WINDOW, waiting for something else bad to happen.

In just a short time, she'd programmed herself to expect the worst. She hated thinking that way, but too many people had been hurt for her not to.

The good news was that, so far, everything appeared fine outside by the gate.

So why had that man sent her that message? Did he want to play games with her?

That's how it appeared.

Her phone buzzed again, and she sucked in a breath.

Was it the man again? Sending her another veiled threat?

But when she looked at the message on her screen, she saw it was from Beckett.

Everything is fine. I'm coming in. Can we talk?

A different kind of apprehension rippled through her. She was glad he was okay.

But she knew what was coming.

The two of them needed to talk. And Sami had to decide how she was going to handle this situation.

She typed back:

Of course. I'll be waiting for you.

But now she needed to gather her thoughts.

And pray for wisdom. Lots and lots of wisdom.

BECKETT HURRIED up the steps to Sami's room and knocked at the door. She answered a moment later.

Warmth spread through him when he saw her. She was seriously the most beautiful woman he had ever seen.

He thought she might return his feelings.

But what if he was wrong? Did he want to take the chance? He'd kept his heart closed for so long. He never thought he'd want to take the risk, not after what he'd seen his parents go through. But Sami made him hope for different possibilities for the future.

"Beckett . . ." She lingered in the doorway. "You're okay. I'm so glad."

"It's been a precarious day, to say the least, but I'm fine." He shifted. "Can I come in for a minute?"

She hesitated for just a second before opening the door wider. "Of course."

They walked toward her couch and sat down.

Beckett had always been a direct kind of guy, and this conversation would be no different.

He took a deep breath before starting. "Listen, I thought there was something between us. But if I overstepped, then I want to apologize."

Sami drew in a deep breath, as if trying to figure out how to respond.

Beckett had hoped for a quick rejection of what he said, a "No, you're not wrong. I felt it too."

But that didn't come.

"I'm sorry, Beckett." She raked a hand through her hair before letting out a long breath. "I think I just got carried away in the moment. Maybe we both did. It's the situation. It's playing on our emotions, making everything feel heightened. Almost losing your life can do that to a person and . . ." She shrugged as if she didn't know what else to say.

His pulse throbbed in his ears. "Is that how you feel?"

She pulled her gaze up to meet his. "I'm not usually given to whims, so I'm not sure what came over me. But today I realized that I shouldn't have kissed you like that."

"I see." Beckett's voice hardened.

Sami glanced at her hands, her downturned mouth and bent posture showing regret. "I'm sorry, Beckett. I'm usually much more careful than this, more guarded."

Guarded? Was that what she called it?

"Usually, you only guard something you want to protect," he finally said.

"Then I guess I'm trying to protect my heart."

"Are you afraid I'm going to break it?"

She swallowed hard before rubbing her throat. "I . . . we . . . we're not . . ."

He waited for Sami to finish. But she was obviously at a loss for words. Her mouth opened and shut before she finally shook her head.

Was this really because she didn't think he was good enough for her?

That seemed clear.

He stood, realizing that there was nothing left to say.

"I'll keep my distance," he muttered.

Sami didn't return his feelings. She didn't owe him an explanation either. One kiss didn't demand that.

"Beckett . . ." She rubbed her throat as she glanced up at him. She looked like she wanted to say more. Or maybe even like she regretted what she'd already said.

He waited for her to finish. To explain. To prove his theory wrong.

But she didn't.

Instead, he stood and stepped to the door. "I hope this doesn't change the fact that I'm going to need to help protect you."

"Of course not," she rushed. "We're both professional. I'm sure we'll be just fine."

He stared at her another moment before nodding. "Great. Because we're all going to reconvene in two hours. Can you meet us in the conference room then?"

"I'll be there." She nodded, even though her gaze still looked strained.

Suddenly, he couldn't wait to have this assignment over with.

The sooner, the better.

Once this was wrapped up, Sami could return to her life back in Atlanta, and Beckett could continue working here.

And he could pretend like none of this had ever happened.

But he knew that would be easier said than done.

CHAPTER THIRTY-ONE

"YOU TOLD BECKETT THAT?" Elise gawked at Sami as they sat together on the couch in Elise's apartment.

Sami had desperately needed someone to talk to. But now, she frowned at her friend's overblown expression of outrage.

"Why do I feel like I've grown a third eye?" Sami asked before taking another sip of her coffee.

"Because you have!" Elise rubbed her belly and leaned back into the cushions. "You and Beckett have chemistry. Everyone can see it. I thought you might actually give him a chance."

"It would never work." Sami shrugged. "I deal with couples whose relationships are on the rocks all the time. As you know, if people marry more than once, they usually marry their opposite the first time. If they get married again, they marry their equal."

"Okay . . ." Elise scrunched her eyes as if confused where she was going with this.

"Beckett and I are total opposites, and I've seen too many marriages fall apart. I don't want to be one of them, and the odds are stacked against us."

"How?"

Sami threw her hands in the air. "So many reasons. First of all, Beckett's not my type."

"Tall, hunky, and kind isn't your type?"

Sami felt her cheeks flush. "I mean, maybe. But it shouldn't be. I really need to marry someone who's more like me. Someone whose job isn't doing tactical operations. Who has a nine-to-five job."

"That's silly."

Sami froze. This wasn't what she'd expected to hear from her friend. She'd thought Elise would understand. Her friend was down-to-earth, and they almost always saw eye to eye on things.

"The two of us are just not compatible!" Sami finally blurted.

"Says who?"

Sami crossed her arms. "Says every personality test I've ever taken or given."

Elise pressed her lips together in thought before finally speaking. "But, Sami, there comes a point where you have to trust your gut. It's not all about textbooks and studies."

"But feelings are deceitful. You and I both know that."

Elise raised her hands. "I know, I know. Believe me, I do. I just want you to be more open-minded. Maybe you'll find the two of you are much more compatible than you ever thought. In fact, you might find you're much more alike than you can imagine."

"You're rooting for me to fall in love, aren't you?" Sami stared at her friend, watching her every expression.

Elise shrugged, not denying it. "Maybe I am. I know how happy the right relationship can make you."

"Yes, you do, don't you?" Elise had been married twice, both times to wonderful men. Her first husband had been killed during a SEAL operation where he'd sacrificed himself to save others. He'd been Colton's best friend.

"Sami, you see the worst sides of relationships," Elise said. "People come to you when they're at the point of everything falling apart. But there are plenty of other people who don't feel that way."

She let her friend's words sink in for a minute. "On a logical level, I know you're right. But maybe I've programmed myself to think every relationship ends with heartache. I certainly see enough of it. I thought I'd protected myself from those pitfalls, but maybe I haven't."

"It can happen to the best of us. Besides, there's one other thing you don't know about Beckett." Elise stared at Sami, her eyes dancing with unspoken revelations.

"What's that? Does he secretly smile at you?" Her humor covered up the fact that Sami was actually honored he'd smiled and broken down his own walls.

"Beckett has always said he only wants to fall in love once."

Sami froze. That wasn't what she'd expected to hear. "What?"

Elise nodded. "That's right. He's never married because he's so picky. He said he's never met the right woman, and he's holding out for Ms. Right."

"And you think I could be Ms. Right?" Doubt tinged Sami's voice.

Elise shrugged. "I think it's a good possibility."

BECKETT FIRED his gun at the range they had on the Blackout grounds.

After his earlier neuropathy, he needed to get some of his frustration out—and prove that he was still the best sharpshooter around.

But with every shot, his thoughts went back to Sami.

How could he have misread the woman so badly? He knew he had bigger worries at hand than a relationship at this moment. Yet his thoughts couldn't seem to stray from the beautiful stranger he'd found in that tower. She'd turned his life upside down in so many ways—good ways.

He remembered their most recent conversation.

Or not.

He fired again, this time hitting the bull's eye.

Maybe he could put his mind at ease now—at least partially.

He glanced at the time before putting his gun away and heading back inside for his next meeting. Maybe he'd be able to focus a little more now.

A few minutes later, he took his place at the conference table. Someone had brought in a platter of sandwiches, chips, and fruit. Beckett grabbed an apple and a bottle of water.

When Sami stepped into the room, his breath caught.

Sami was the first woman he'd been interested in in a long time. He prided himself on reading people. He'd thought she felt the same interest in him. Yet he had been wrong.

She glanced at him before quickly looking away and taking the seat beside him.

Now that she was here, the meeting could start.

Colton stood at the front of the room. "I have several updates for everyone. First of all, there's still no news on Ernie. Nobody has seen him. Cassidy and her crew are investigating Ernie's disappearance. Until we know more, we need to treat this as if Ernie's disappearance is tied with this case. And if Ernie is missing because of something that's happening here, then the stakes have become even greater. We have to find him before somebody else is hurt."

Beckett couldn't agree more. "I think we need to review everything that we know so far. The answers are somewhere in those details."

"Exactly what I was going to suggest next."

Colton crossed his arms, exhaustion pulling at his features.

Probably just as it pulled at all of their features. The past few days had been a whirlwind of danger and tragedy.

"First, Sami was abducted and placed in a tower in the mountains," Colton started. "While she was trapped, two people were killed and clues were left pointing us toward finding her. Next, that bomb was dropped onto our campus using a drone."

"But before the bomb was dropped, I got that text message saying, 'Can I come inside.'" Sami grabbed an orange and began peeling it.

"Yes, that's right. Those texts tie into this somehow also, even though we haven't gotten a hit on the location of the sender." Colton paused and glanced at his notes. "After the bomb went off, you got a text saying, 'You should have let me in,' correct?"

Sami nodded and plucked an orange slice from the rest of the fruit. "That's right."

"Next, we found the body in the rug and then someone unleashed dogs on Sami," Colton said.

Beckett felt his muscles tense as he pictured the scene playing out again. That whole situation had been close. Too close.

"And as if this wasn't enough already, Ernie is missing, and we found a camera hidden on a tree in the woods."

"Don't forget the inhaler I found and the person shooting at me," Beckett turned to Sami. "Whoever is behind this may have asthma. We're still waiting to see if we get a DNA hit on it."

"I also got another text today." Sami frowned and grabbed a napkin to wipe her hands. "It said, 'Are you expecting guests?'"

"And we discovered that three of the victims all lived in Atlanta at the same time," Beckett added.

"Is there anything else that I didn't cover?" Colton glanced around the room.

"Don't forget the doll, the dog collar, and the piece of bread outside the gate today. I took a picture and documented today's find, just in case." Beckett pulled it up on his phone and showed everybody.

As he did, Sami sucked in a breath.

Everyone turned toward her to see what her reaction was about.

"Did you remember something?" Beckett narrowed his gaze as he waited for her answer.

Sami's eyes wavered back and forth as if she was processing something. Then her gaze found Gabe. "The bomb that was left on the campus, the one left by the drone . . . did you say it looked like a tinderbox?"

Gabe nodded. "I did. Why?"

She let out a long breath before running a hand over her face. "How did I not see this before?"

CHAPTER THIRTY-TWO

SAMI'S THOUGHTS continued to race as she sat at the conference table, reeling from the picture coming together in her mind. How could she have missed the clues? They'd been right in front of her the whole time.

"Sami . . .?"

Beckett's voice pulled her out of her thoughts.

She shook her head and tried to gather herself before glancing around the table. She hoped her theory didn't sound too outlandish.

"See if my line of reasoning makes any sense." She pressed her lips together before saying, "I think the man who abducted me is trying to recreate children's stories."

Beckett squinted beside her. "Can you spell out your thought process more?"

"Of course. Me being left in a tower? Rapunzel. The dog collar sent to my father, combined with the tinderbox bomb and dogs being unleashed? It's from the story 'The Tinderbox' by Hans Christian Anderson."

Axel grunted. "I'm not sure I've heard of that one."

"In a nutshell, a soldier finds a tinderbox, and it releases three hounds that will do the man's bidding," Sami explained.

"I both like and dislike where you're going with this," Colton said. "Please continue."

"Even the first text that was sent to me . . . it was a line from the 'Three Little Pigs.' The wolf said, 'Let me in.' The text sent to me today? I'm not 100 percent sure where it's from, but I think it may be 'Hansel and Gretel.'"

"Then somebody left a piece of bread by the gate, which would signify breadcrumbs . . . For that matter, he's been leaving breadcrumbs behind all along, hasn't he?" Beckett rubbed his beard as his gaze hardened. "You're right—how didn't we see this theme earlier? But good job figuring it out."

She wasn't sure how they'd missed this. But facts

continued to zip through her mind and click into place. "You said one woman died and was left in her bed? Could this guy have been trying to recreate 'Sleeping Beauty'?"

"I won't rule anything out right now," Colton said.

"The man who was pushed from the treehouse in his backyard? 'Jack and the Beanstalk,'" Sami continued. "Even the man found rolled in the area rug . . . maybe he's supposed to signify 'Aladdin.' It could be a stretch, but think about it. All the murders were so strange. Maybe this is why."

Silence filled the room as everyone absorbed her words.

Finally, Colton nodded slowly, his jaw hardened. "I agree that it's an eerie connection. But everything seems to make sense now. Still, even if this is what our perp is doing, why? What is this person trying to convey? Sami, do you have any insight into this as a psychologist?"

Her thoughts continued to race, to formulate, to piece together the mystery of the human mind and motivations. The person behind this has laid out all the clues—but they were so outlandish that it had been hard to link—even though it all had been right in front of their eyes.

There was one more thing that she needed to mention . . . "There's only one thing I can add right now. I don't think that this is about my father at all."

"Then who's it about?" Gabe narrowed his eyes with confusion.

"This is about . . . me." Her voice trailed as guilt gnawed at her.

Beckett shifted to fully face her. Doubt and concern filled his gaze. "Why would you say that?"

"Because I use children's stories when I work with children. What if one of my past clients is trying to teach me a lesson?"

"A past client from, let's say, ten years ago?" Beckett asked.

Her grim expression met his. "I'd say that's a good guess."

BECKETT LET Sami's theory roll around in his mind. He hated to admit it, but her words made sense. Still, they had a lot to figure out concerning this case.

"So . . . this guy is leaving literal breadcrumbs for us now," Beckett muttered. The person behind these crimes certainly had a twisted imagination.

Colton leaned back in his seat, his gaze still hard with thought. "If Sami's theory is correct then that makes the most sense."

"So how do we find the rest of the bread-crumbs?" Rocco glanced around the room at each of his teammates.

Sami let out a long breath before saying, "I'm guessing he leaves them for us as soon as he sees fit."

Beckett frowned and shook his head. There was only one positive he could see coming from this scenario. "And if that's true, that means he's still on the island."

"And he could have Ernie," Rocco added.

Colton's shoulders stiffened. "If Ernie's on this island, then we need to find him. I'm guessing that those breadcrumbs this guy is leaving will eventually lead us to him."

"But I worry that by the time we find Ernie it's going to be too late." Beckett hated to be the one who said it, but his words were true. Considering three people were already dead, they had no time to waste.

Sami's phone buzzed, and she glanced down at it. "I have another text from that unknown number. It says, 'Come out, come out, wherever you are.'"

Colton shook his head and squinted. "I've heard that before, but what story is it from?"

Sami frowned as she thought about it a moment. "I think it's originally used in Hide-and-Seek, the game. But maybe it's also used in the *The Wizard of Oz*."

"I think you're right," Beckett said.

"Is this guy trying to goad us into leaving the campus?" Colton squinted before shaking his head.

"There's no telling," Sami said. "I wish I had more answers . . . but we're getting closer."

CHAPTER THIRTY-THREE

"BECKETT, I want you to work with Sami and make a list of any potential clients who could be behind this," Colton said. "Especially note any who had asthma—if that's even something you remember, Sami."

"But there's the matter of client confidentiality." Sami's voice trailed. "I can't disclose information about them without a warrant."

"Tell us whatever you can. I don't want you to lose your license. But I also don't want you to lose your life."

Colton's words caused her to suck in a breath. That clearly wasn't what she wanted either. But she hated being in this kind of situation. She didn't want to have to choose between living or breaking a professional trust.

"That's one more reason I want you to work only with Beckett right now. It can be between the two of you, and you don't have to present anything to the group that you're not comfortable with. Meanwhile, the rest of us are going to continue looking for Ernie."

"Quick thought: Are there any updates on the dogs?" Gabe straightened and glanced at Colton. "Did we figure out who they belong to? Were they micro-chipped? Maybe they're a clue of some type."

Colton shook his head. "They weren't micro-chipped, and nobody has reported them missing. We're still trying to track down those answers."

Sami glanced at Beckett and felt the heat rising up her neck.

It seemed like the two of them were going to be spending a lot of time together. Just yesterday, that thought would have thrilled her. Right now, all she could think about was that awkward conversation she'd had with him earlier.

Elise's words wouldn't leave her mind either. Sami had a lot to think about, and it was nearly impossible to think through anything with Beckett being so close. What she needed was space.

But space wasn't something that she was going to get right now.

Instead, Sami needed to think back through all her past cases and see if she could figure out which one of her former clients might be behind these heinous acts.

BECKETT GLANCED across his office at Sami, sensing that she felt the tension between them.

Despite their earlier conversation, he still felt a need to protect her. He wished there was something he could say to make her feel better—even though she was the one who'd stomped on his heart.

Sami did care about him—even if she denied it. Beckett knew there was something between them. She must have her own reasons for being resistant, and he didn't want to push. The last thing he wanted was to entangle himself in a relationship that would go nowhere.

Sami showed him a list of names she'd been scribbling.

Beckett moved closer so he could see the paper. As he did, a zing rushed through him. Her sweet scent drifted over him, and for a moment he thought about the kiss they'd shared. But he pushed away the emotions.

He needed to focus right now.

"These were clients I've worked with during that timeframe who possibly had the capacity for murder. I don't want to think that any of my past clients could be guilty of this," Sami explained. "But I don't want to be naive either."

Beckett stared at the list.

Bryon Simons.

William Harkness.

Rick Wolfe.

"Can you tell me anything about these people?" he asked.

"All of these clients had been in their early teens. They'd come from troubled backgrounds. And they'd been resistant to therapy." She let out a long breath. "Byron . . . he watched someone shoot his older brother outside his house. William . . . his parents were alcoholics, and they fought so much he was put into foster care at five. Rick . . . his parents ignored him. He turned to harming himself to try to get attention."

"That's tough. Really tough."

She nodded. "These cases were all when I did an

internship also. I was just beginning my doctorate program so I wasn't fully licensed yet."

"Tell me about how these children's stories might be tied to you."

"I use stories as a part of my therapy." She sighed and leaned back in her chair. "So many stories teach deeper lessons. Plus, the act of reading together can make children feel more secure. Stories can be a wonderful thing and make you realize that you're not all alone in the world."

"So all these stories that have been recreated are ones that you've used?" Beckett glanced at her.

Sami nodded and scooted back—just slightly. "But you have to understand that I've seen hundreds of clients. Without getting into any personal details, I can maybe narrow any possible suspects down to these few people with proclivities toward possible violence. Based on the victims, we can narrow it down to an eighteen-month period also."

Beckett rubbed a hand over his beard. "Who decides when therapy sessions should end?"

"Sometimes, I do if I feel comfortable that the problems have been resolved. Even when that happens, my clients sometimes want to keep seeing me to make sure they stay on track. Other times, a client or the client's parent might decide he or she wants to stop coming. Sometimes it's because they don't believe the therapy is helping or maybe they think it's too expensive."

"Are those the main reasons?"

"On occasion, one of my clients will end up in a juvenile detention center or jail. I don't continue treating them when that happens."

"Have any of your clients ever threatened you?"

She seemed to think about it for a moment before shaking her head. "Not really. Have I had a few who've been upset with me? Sure. That's the nature of my job. Some clients want to see faster progress or for me to sign a form saying they're all done when they clearly aren't. But I've never had any clients who have taken it further than that."

Beckett stared at the names she had listed. "So these people right here are the only ones you think have a bent toward violence?"

She frowned but nodded. "If I had to narrow it down, it would be to these people."

"Then we're going to need to look into their backgrounds and see if they have alibis during these crimes."

"I understand. As long as we can keep this on the down low until we know anything for sure."

"Of course."

Just then, Rocco stepped into the room with his phone in his hands. "We found more slices of bread."

Beckett raised his head, his eyes lighting with curiosity. "Did they lead to anything?"

"They did. They formed a trail, leading to a house."

"Whose?" Sami's word hung in the air.

"You'll never believe this," Rocco continued, a hint of trepidation in his voice. "But it turns out Wilson Davis never left the island after all."

Beckett's breath caught. "Is that right?"

"Yes, it is. The police are going to bring him in for questioning."

Beckett nodded slowly. "That sounds like a great idea."

And he wanted to be there when that happened.

CHAPTER THIRTY-FOUR

WILSON? Could he be behind this? Yet he'd never been Sami's client.

Why had he secretly stayed on the island?

The questions raced through her head.

"We'll question him first." Rocco lingered in the doorway. "You guys keep working through those names. Any progress?"

Sami glanced at Beckett's desk in front of her and at the list she'd put together. She held up the paper. "I have some names."

"We're going to start looking into each of these people," Beckett added. "We thought it would be better if we kept the initial information between the two of us, like Colton suggested."

"Good idea—at least until you can narrow it down. Let me know if you discover anything."

"Will do," Beckett said.

Beckett slid a computer across the desk toward Sami. "Let's start with social media and see if we can figure out if any potential suspects have solid alibis like being out of the country and such. We'll go from there."

Sami worked on it for the next two hours. Two people she'd listed had ended up in jail. One was now a missionary in South America. Another had just been awarded teacher of the year—and had plenty of photos from his hometown in Illinois to give him an alibi.

That left only one more name before they were all eliminated.

What she really wanted was to hear an update on Wilson. She couldn't stop thinking about his presence on the island.

Finally, Rocco came in with an update.

"Wilson claims he stayed on the island because he needed a break from the political climate surrounding Judge Reynolds' latest case back in Georgia."

"Then why did he say he was leaving?" Sami asked.

"Wilson was afraid you'd report back to your father if you knew he decided to stay."

Sami shook her head, trying to understand the man's reasoning. "What did he tell my father?"

"That he wasn't feeling well and wouldn't be able to make the trip."

Sami rubbed her temples as she felt a headache coming on. "He's obviously prone to lying. Do you think that he could be behind what's happening?"

"He would be an easy suspect," Beckett said. "That is for sure. But he was with your father when you were abducted. They were both working late that night."

She stared at the final name on her list.

As she picked up her phone to do some research, she noted how warm the metal felt.

The next instant, the device exploded in her hands.

She screamed as fire and smoke filled the air.

"IT LOOKS like you're going to be just fine." Doctor Autumn Spenser stepped back from the exam table and smiled. "But that was a close call."

Sami rubbed the stitches on her arm, thankful it wasn't anything more serious. "Tell me about it."

The phone had exploded in her hands, but thankfully Sami just needed six stitches to close the wound. Some balm had been applied on her palm for minor burns.

Still, it could have been much worse.

Thankfully, Beckett was okay also. He was waiting outside her room now.

Dr. Spenser paused, not in a hurry to leave. "How's your stress level?"

The doctor had beautiful auburn hair, a slim build, and a great smile.

Sami immediately felt at ease with her—even as the scent of the Lantern Beach Medical Clinic surrounded her.

Sami let out a breath, wondering exactly how much she should say. "It's okay. But I'd be lying if I said this whole situation hasn't turned my world upside down."

The doctor's lips turned down with compassion. "I can only imagine. Just try to take it easy. You've been through a lot. But I'm sure you know that. I hear you're a psychologist."

"Unfortunately, it's easier to give advice than it is to take it."

"That's the way it usually works." The doctor cast a smile. "How long will you be staying here?"

That was a good question. Something that Sami needed to figure out also. "I suppose that as soon as it's safe for me to go home, I will. However, if this continues to stretch on then I'm going to have to make some difficult choices."

"Just be careful. I know when you're in a position where you're called to help other people, it's often easy to neglect yourself. But we've both seen the repercussions of doing that. So make sure you take care of yourself."

Sami nodded. "I'll do my best. I hear you're a newcomer on the island."

"I am," the doctor said. "I haven't been here long. But so far, I'm loving it. If only I could keep the Blackout guys from coming here so often."

Sami let out a chuckle. "Thankfully, it hasn't been for anything too serious yet, right?"

"Absolutely." Dr. Spenser stepped toward the door. "You come back if you need anything, you hear? Anything at all."

"Will do." But part of Sami didn't want the doctor to go. Because she knew as soon as Dr. Spenser was gone, Sami was going to have to spend more time with Beckett.

Not that being with him was a bad thing.

But she felt the tension thrumming between them. It wasn't just normal tension, either. It was intense tension. Heavy tension.

Tension that couldn't be ignored.

And she wasn't exactly sure what she should do about it.

CHAPTER THIRTY-FIVE

BECKETT FELT his heart skip a beat when he saw Sami step from the examination room. A bandage had been wrapped around her forearm, but that was all.

Things could have turned out much worse.

He swallowed hard as Sami paused in front him. A knot formed in his throat at the thought of how close Sami had come to a more serious injury.

How in the world had her cell phone exploded? He'd never seen anything like it.

Hopefully, they'd have some answers soon.

"All good to go?" he asked.

Sami nodded and touched her arm. "The doctor said I'll be just fine."

"That's good news."

Beckett hated the stilted conversation between them, but he would take what he could get right now.

They started down the hallway together.

"Anything new?" Sami asked. "Do you guys know how that happened to my phone?"

"They're looking at it now. Colton wants to know when your phone was left unattended."

She paused and let out a breath. "It's usually with me all the time. I keep it in my pocket. The last time I remember not having it on me was when I was abducted."

"What happened to it when this guy abducted you?"

"I dropped it in my car when he grabbed me. The police found it there when they searched for me."

Beckett frowned.

"You think this guy went back and planted something in my phone after he abducted me?" Sami asked.

He shrugged. "Honestly? It's my best guess. An explosive. Maybe even a tracker."

She shivered and crossed her arms over her chest.

Beckett scanned the area in front of him to make

sure danger wasn't lingering. He saw nothing of concern. But he needed to remain on guard.

"I feel sick about this whole situation . . . especially knowing it's my fault."

Beckett froze, concern filling him. His gaze connected with Sami's, and determination filled him —determination to help Sami see things in a different light.

"It's not your fault, Sami," he started. "You didn't make this guy do this."

She nibbled on her bottom lip, looking unconvinced. "The fact that it all goes back to me gives me some culpability. People have gotten hurt, and I can't say that I have nothing to do with that."

"Sami . . ." There was so much he wanted to say.

But when he saw her suck in a breath and drag her gaze up to meet his, he clamped his mouth shut. She was trying to sort this out on her own terms.

"I would like to look more into the deaths of the three people who were killed while I was abducted. I know there's a link between them and one of my past clients. I'd like to dig a little deeper and see if I've missed anything."

"Of course."

She nodded. "How about if we head back to your headquarters then?"

Keeping her at Blackout headquarters sounded like a good idea. Even this short trip to the clinic had been risky. If Beckett had his way, he would keep Sami inside that building until this was resolved. But even that hadn't proven to be safe.

Beckett wished he could find a good solution.

But their only solution right now was to find this guy and stop him before he destroyed any more lives.

SAMI'S THOUGHTS continued to race as she and Beckett headed down the road in a car he'd borrowed from Colton. His truck tires still hadn't been replaced.

She tried to remember everything she'd learned about the three people who'd been killed since this craziness had begun. If she recalled correctly one was a social worker, another a retired teacher, and the third a construction worker.

Though their names didn't sound familiar, Sami knew they were somehow connected. They'd narrowed down the year, and she'd gone through the names of her past clients from that specific time period. But there were still links they were missing.

If she'd been in therapy with a child going through a rough time—maybe even a child who was in the foster care system—then this person could have easily been connected with a teacher or a social worker. Maybe all along those people's identities should have been offering clues to her.

But just as easily as her thoughts focused on those things, they also bounced back to Beckett. It seemed as if God was trying to speak to her. First, He'd used Elise. Now, He had used Dr. Autumn Spenser.

It was true that it was often easier to take care of others than it was to take care of yourself. Maybe she'd been neglecting her own emotional needs for far too long.

And maybe she should just be open and tell Beckett a little bit more about her struggle. Was it fair to keep him in the dark? Especially after they'd shared such a strong bond last night.

Beckett only wants to fall in love once.

Elise's words echoed through Sami's head.

She knew she'd be a fool to push Beckett away. He was worth the risk, worth taking a chance.

"Beckett . . ." She licked her lips as she tried to gather the courage to start.

"Yes?" He gave her a quick glance before returning his eyes to the road.

"I know I've been acting and reacting strangely. I just want you to know that—"

A screech filled the air. She looked over just in time to see a large vehicle barreling toward them.

Then she heard the sound of metal crunching. Glass breaking. Beckett shouting.

They'd been T-boned, hadn't they?

Before Sami could comprehend the scope of what had just happened, pain erupted and everything went black.

CHAPTER THIRTY-SIX

BECKETT'S EARS RANG.

His body ached.

His vision blurred.

Was he back on the battlefield? Had an IED just exploded?

His mind drifted back in time. At once, he could smell the dusty ground beneath him. Hear the footsteps of his colleagues as they ran for cover. Feel the bullets whizzing past.

His mind played tricks on him.

"Beckett! Beckett!" a voice called in the distance.

He blinked several times, willing his head to stop spinning.

But everything around him felt like a blur.

Except for . . .

What was that smell?

Was it . . . gasoline?

His eyes popped open.

That was right.

He'd been driving down the road when someone T-boned him.

Sami . . .

He jerked his head to the right, ignoring the pain in his neck.

He needed to know that Sami was okay.

But an empty passenger seat stared back.

Empty?

"We need to get you out of here," a familiar voice said.

Was that . . . Rocco?

Beckett turned, wishing his head would clear. His vision. That his ears would stop ringing.

He thought he saw Rocco through the haze surrounding his window.

"I heard the crash all the way at Blackout." Rocco jerked on the door, his motions quick but urgent. "This car could blow. We have to get you out, but the door won't open."

Beckett grabbed the handle and pushed.

But Rocco was right.

The door wouldn't budge.

The impact must have crushed the metal.

"Can you move to the passenger side?" Rocco rushed.

Beckett glanced over again. The still empty seat confirmed he wasn't losing his mind.

"Sami . . .?"

Rocco frowned. "She wasn't here when I got here. I'm going to send some of our guys to search for her. Right now, we need to concentrate on getting you out of this vehicle."

Beckett thought he nodded. He knew as well as anyone that he needed to get out of here.

Not for his own sake.

But so he could find Sami.

He tugged on the seatbelt. It didn't budge.

He tugged again, but it was stuck.

Just then, something popped under the front hood. A plume of smoke rose.

"Beckett, we need to work faster." Urgency raced through Rocco's voice. "We don't have much time."

Beckett reached for the knife in his pocket, hoping he could cut the seatbelt off.

But as another pop sounded from the hood, Beckett was afraid he was too late.

SAMI DRAGGED HER EYES OPEN. She glanced around, but darkness surrounded her.

At once, she remembered the wreck. Remembered being in the car as another vehicle slammed into it.

Beckett.

Where was he? Had he been injured in that car wreck?

The other vehicle had hit his side of the car.

A cry caught in her throat.

Beckett . . . What if he didn't make it?

Sami could hardly bear the thought.

She pushed herself up from the hard floor.

Clearly, this wasn't a hospital.

That's when the truth slammed into her.

Whoever had hit her and Beckett with that vehicle had done so on purpose. He'd done so to hurt Beckett and give himself the opportunity to grab Sami.

The person behind this had abducted her again.

Nausea pooled in her stomach at the thought.

Where was she?

She waited a few minutes for her eyes to adjust to the darkness.

She appeared to be in a room of some sort. There

were no windows, just a rough wooden floor beneath her and one door against the opposite wall.

What were the chances it was unlocked?

Not great.

Sami tried to drag herself to her feet, but it didn't work.

Her body ached too much right now.

She did a quick self-assessment. She didn't think any bones were broken. She was probably just sore from the impact.

But that wasn't her biggest worry right now.

Right now, she had to concentrate on getting out of here.

Because what if Beckett needed her help, just like she needed his?

CHAPTER THIRTY-SEVEN

"WHERE COULD SHE BE?" Beckett asked.

Colton and Rocco stood with him near the wrecked vehicle. Smoke still came from the hood, and the burning odor of scorched metal and rubber filled the air. The explosion had charred the car and blasted out the windshield.

Cassidy and her crew were on the scene investigating as well as the Lantern Beach Fire Department.

Beckett had made it out of the car before it exploded, though just barely.

He was thankful to be alive right now. He had a scratch on his arm, and no doubt he'd be sore.

All things considered, he was doing great.

But he wouldn't rest until he knew Sami was okay also.

It was clear by the tire prints left behind that someone had charged at Beckett and Sami, coming full speed toward them from a side street. This person must have been driving a larger vehicle in order to flee the scene. The driver somehow knew Beckett and Sami would come by here after they left the clinic.

Anger fisted inside Beckett at the thought.

This whole thing had been planned.

Somebody had been waiting for the moment Beckett and Sami came past to do this.

All so he could grab Sami.

It was probably the only way this person had been able to think of to get her away from Beckett.

"We have everybody out there looking for her, and we tried to follow the tire prints," Rocco said.

"This guy is too smart to be caught like that." Beckett frowned and rubbed his beard. "We're not going to find him that way."

"We're doing everything we can."

Beckett let out a long breath. "I know. I know you are. I'm not trying to come down hard on you. It's just that . . ."

Colton clutched his shoulder. "I know. I get it. We're going to find her."

Beckett glanced at his watch. "It's probably been forty-five minutes since this person grabbed her. Who knows where they are now?"

"If they are on this island then we'll find them," Colton said. "We'll go door-to-door if that's what we have to do."

Beckett nodded.

There was no way he could just stand around here and wait for other people to do this.

He needed to get out there and find Sami himself.

Then he wanted to hear what she'd started to say right before the truck rammed them.

FINALLY, Sami dragged herself to her feet.

Just as she'd thought, her entire body ached. But she needed to push through that pain.

She started to the door when she spotted a paper on the floor with a small flashlight beside it. Quickly, she snatched them both up and twisted the flashlight on.

A message written in thick, large letters stared back.

You can go in every room except the one at the end of the hall.

A chill went through her.

This was another children's story, she realized. Where had she heard this before?

Bluebeard.

That was right. The man got married more than once, and each time he told his new wife that she could go anywhere in her new house except one room. When the wife opened the door to the forbidden room, she found the bodies of his other dead wives inside.

That wasn't the sanitized children's version of the story.

But that was the way the tale had originally been written.

If Sami opened the door at the end of the hallway, what would she find inside? Or who?

Beckett's image filled her mind, and she held back a gasp.

Please, Lord. No . . .

But she couldn't stay in this room. Not if she

didn't have to. She had to figure out how to get out of here. Had to know if Beckett was okay.

Her leg ached as she moved forward. The accident had obviously exacerbated her injured ankle.

She limped toward the door and twisted the handle.

To her surprise, it opened.

She held her breath as she glanced out into the dark hallway.

The sun had been setting when she and Beckett had been driving home from the clinic. It must be dark outside now. Eerily dark.

How much time had passed?

She wasn't sure.

Just like she wasn't sure if she really wanted to know what waited for her once she left this room.

She had no choice but to find out.

CHAPTER THIRTY-EIGHT

BECKETT COULDN'T STOP PACING. He'd driven all over this island himself. Had searched down the side roads.

But really all he was doing was wasting time.

He felt helpless to find Sami, and feeling helpless wasn't acceptable.

There *had* to be a way to locate her. He just needed to figure out what that was.

Gabe and Rocco were tracking down the last person on Sami's list.

If one of those people was behind this, maybe they could track that person down. Ping their cell phone.

Something.

But everything took time, and time was something they didn't have.

Beckett looked up as Gabe darted into the conference room. His eyes sparkled as if he had news. "I think I found something."

Beckett stepped closer. "What's that?"

"I've been looking at the list of Sami's former clients," he started. "I decided to look into all of them, instead of only the three she narrowed it down to. And I found someone who changed his name a few years back."

"Okay . . ." Beckett waited for whatever Gabe would say next.

"I also found a present-day connection between this person and Sami." Gabe shook his head. "I can't believe we didn't see this earlier."

"Who is it?" Beckett braced himself for the answer.

SAMI SQUINTED as a figure came into view at the end of the hallway.

"Are you going into that room?" a deep voice asked.

The tones sounded familiar. But the man was shadowed, and Sami couldn't make out any details.

"I don't know." Sami took a step back and ran into the wall. There was nowhere for her to go—except forward or back into the room where she'd woken up. "What will I find inside?"

"You'll have to open the door to see."

"What if I don't want to open that door?"

"Then I guess we'll never know."

She pressed her hands against the wall, not wanting to move away from it. How was she going to get out of this? Clearly, she couldn't run.

That meant she was going to have to do what she was best at: talking to people.

Or actually listening would be better.

She needed to get this guy talking, try and discover what he had planned, and see if she could get him to change his mind. She knew it was a long shot, but what other choice did she have right now?

None.

"Why did you bring me here?" Her voice trembled as she asked the question.

"Because you needed to be taught a lesson." Anger simmered beneath his voice.

She had to keep this guy's emotions under control

before he unleashed them on her. "I get it that you're angry with me. But why go through all this trouble? You've really gone out of your way for me."

"You still don't know yet, do you?" Disgust—and a touch of smugness—dripped from every word.

"Know what?"

"Who I am."

She had a feeling she'd insult him if she said no. Instead, she had to talk her way around this, if possible. "You're somebody I used to meet with for therapy."

"That's right. For the longest time, I thought that you were the only person who cared about me."

Her heart pounded in her ears as his words settled in her mind. "I care about all my clients."

"But not enough to keep up with them once they're out of the system." His voice rose with every word.

Sami's throat went dry as she realized just how deeply this man's emotional trauma went. She had to convince him to see things from her perspective. But this would be an uphill battle.

"I don't have much choice in that," she tried to explain. "It wouldn't be very professional of me to go track people down on my own time."

"Is that right?" Cynicism stained his tone. "But

it's not nice of you to make people think that you care when you really don't."

Sami's heart continued to pound in her ears. This man had clearly formed an unhealthy attachment to her, thinking their relationship was more than professional.

How could she convince him that she'd cared even though she hadn't stayed in contact?

"I'm not sure I understand what you are talking about," she murmured. "Can you tell me more?"

The figure stepped closer. As he did, his face came into view.

Full cheeks. Dark hair. A pointy nose. A fit build.

Sami sucked in a breath.

It was . . . her neighbor.

Dan Blake.

"Dan?" She tried to put what she knew together. But the facts still didn't make sense. "I don't understand."

His expression darkened. "No, and that's been the problem all along."

CHAPTER THIRTY-NINE

AS THE NAME rolled around in Beckett's head, he strode toward the phone at the end of the conference table.

"I'm going to call this guy's wife." Beckett grabbed his computer and found the information he needed. A moment later, he picked up the phone and punched in the number.

He put the device on speaker so everybody could hear.

A woman answered a moment later.

"Hello, Mrs. Blake," Beckett started. "My name is Beckett Jones, and I'm trying to reach your husband."

"Dan? Don't you have his cell phone number?"

"I'm afraid he's not answering. Or that I wrote it

down incorrectly. Would you mind giving it to me again?"

"No, not at all." She rattled off the number, and he jotted it down.

Rocco took the paper and hurried to his own computer to run it.

"Look, I need to level with you," Beckett continued. "I'm with a private security group, and we're trying to find your husband. We fear that he could be in danger."

She gasped. "What? What do you mean?"

"I'm afraid I can't go into very many details yet. But it's of the upmost importance that we find him. Do you have any idea where he might be?"

"You're an investigator, you said?"

"That's right." Beckett paused. "This is important, ma'am."

"He went out of town on business." Fear claimed her voice, and her tone pitched upward.

"Tell me again what he does."

"He's an engineer."

"What kind?" Beckett asked.

"He currently specializes in surveying property."

Another question slammed into his mind. "Does he by chance use a drone to do that?"

"Yes, as a matter of fact he does. Why do you want to know that?"

Beckett's gaze met his colleagues. "Just curious. One more question. What about his vehicle? What exactly does he drive?"

"A GMC truck. How does that fit with this?"

"We're still trying to put all the pieces together."

"I'm scared. Is there anything you can tell me?"

"I'm afraid I can't share anything else yet. But I'll let you know when I can."

"My husband . . ." Her voice trembled. "He's a good man. You need to help him. I don't know what's going on, but he doesn't deserve to go through this."

Beckett's stomach clenched. Neither did Sami. She didn't deserve this either.

SAMI CONTINUED to stare at her neighbor, still trying to put the pieces together.

She knew there was more to his story. More to who he was.

What was she missing?

"Picture me skinnier," he said. "With acne. Over-sized clothes. A strong country accent."

She tried to do that, but she still didn't have any

answers.

"Think about one of your clients who still liked to suck his thumb well beyond his toddler years. A client who didn't want to get rid of his security blanket until he was in his teens. Does that ring any bells?"

Realization spread through her. How could she have missed this? Yet the man in front of her seemed like a totally different person . . . even the way he carried himself was different. How he spoke. Dressed. Presented himself.

"Tim Carter . . ." Sami muttered. "I . . . I can't believe this. I can't believe it's you."

"You can call me Dan." His eyes remained narrowed with disgust. "I'm not sure why you're so surprised."

"Of course I'm surprised. There were no signs that you would do something like this. You made great progress when I worked with you."

Tim's name hadn't even ended up on the top of her list. The boy hadn't had proclivities to violence like this. He'd simply been hurting and searching for answers, searching for a way to heal the hurts from his past.

He shrugged. "Things happen when you lose touch."

Sami heard the bitterness in his voice and swallowed hard. This was going to be an uphill battle. She knew by his stance, his eyes, his everything that she wouldn't change his mind on anything.

"Why are you doing this?" she asked instead.

He remained in front of her, something shallow and tepid in his gaze. He didn't even look like the same person who lived beside her. The one with the quiet wife. The one who'd come over for a barbecue once and who got her mail when she was out of town.

"I guess people need to learn lessons," he muttered. "People need to see the invisible."

Sami's throat tightened when she heard the hurt in his voice. "You were never invisible to me."

His nostrils flared. "That's not how it felt. In fact, for a long time I thought you were the only person who cared about me. But then it became evident that you didn't."

"Are you saying that because you moved in next door and I didn't recognize you?"

"Yes!" The word sounded bitter and forceful, and his gaze dripped with resentfulness. "How could you not recognize me when I thought of you practically as a second mother?"

She shook her head, trying to find the right

words that wouldn't trigger him. But she was walking on eggshells, and his emotions had been building up for a long time.

"You look different now than you did when you were younger," she started. "You changed your name. You've grown into a man. Part of you does seem familiar, but I just didn't put the pieces together."

"A real mother would have recognized her son." His voice rose with outrage.

A real mother?

Nausea trickled into Sami's stomach. "Dan . . ."

His face wrinkled with disgust. "It's true. And you know it."

"I'm not your mother," Sami reminded him. "But I did care about you."

"I remember you sat on the couch with me and read me stories."

She licked her lips, trying to remain calm. "So you're trying now to recreate some of those stories from your childhood?"

"I was wondering if you would pick up on that." Sickly satisfaction stretched through his voice. "I did it all for you. I was hoping you'd notice. But it took you too long. I was getting impatient."

"Why kill those other people?"

His eyes gleamed as if he were proud of himself. "They're all people who let me down. My social worker who should have followed up more. An old teacher who always singled me out in class and only wanted to make me feel stupid. A boy from one of my classes who used to make fun of me because I still liked to suck my thumb."

"I understand that those were hard things for you, Dan. You didn't deserve to be treated poorly. But is this really the way you want to continue? Is this the way you want to handle this?"

"Yes! Yes, it is! I've given this a lot of thought. In fact, I've been planning my revenge for a while now. I just had to wait until I learned all the skills I needed before I made my first move."

Sami sensed his rising anger and knew she needed to change the subject. Instead, she glanced at the room at the end of the hallway again. "Dan, you need to tell me what's on the other side of that door."

He snorted. "You're going to have to open it and see for yourself."

A shot of fear rushed through her at the thought. "But . . ."

He raised his gun again. "You're going to do it yourself. Do you understand? And you're going to do it now."

CHAPTER FORTY

"DAN'S PHONE IS OFF." Beckett looked away from his computer, feeling a throb begin in his head.

He'd called their FBI contact to update him, and the feds had run the man's phone number. It hadn't gotten them anywhere.

He wasn't surprised. In fact, he had expected it.

But the update was disappointing, nonetheless.

Another idea hit him, and he straightened. "What's the year of the truck?"

"Let me look." Gabe typed in a few things on the computer. "It's only two years old. Why?"

His pulse raced with possibility. "Because most newer vehicles have a built-in GPS. We might be able to trace his location with that."

"Good idea." Rocco rose. "Let me see what I can

do. I'm going to have to pull some strings in order to make that happen."

Beckett nodded. It seemed like one of their best leads so far.

He wished he could dig into Dan's background and try to find more information that way. But the boy had been a minor when Sami knew him so whatever he might have done would be sealed. But that didn't stop the questions from racing through his head.

Just what was this guy planning on doing with Sami now?

She had been his psychologist. He may have shared some of his deepest, darkest secrets with her. So why did he want to take out his aggression on her now?

The good news was that the man had opportunities to kill Sami before and he hadn't. So maybe he'd keep her alive now. Keep her alive until they found her. Ernie also. They still haven't been able to locate the man.

"I was able to get a location," Rocco said as he strode back into the room.

Beckett's lungs froze. "And?"

"He's here on Lantern Beach."

A whoosh of relief went through him—followed

immediately by a surge of adrenaline. He rushed to his feet, knowing they had no time to waste. "Let's go find him."

———

WHILE DAN HELD the gun to her, Sami walked toward the door and pushed it open.

She gasped when she saw someone lying on the floor, his hands and ankles bound.

"Ernie?" Even thought she'd never seen the man, she instinctively knew who he was. He was the only person who made sense.

As she said his name, he turned his head.

He was still alive!

"Shut the door again," Dan ordered.

She didn't ask any questions and did as he said. At least, she knew Ernie hadn't been killed. It appeared he was simply being held here, but she didn't see any obvious wounds or injuries.

"Why bring Ernie into this?" she asked. "He's innocent."

"I was innocent too, and the world rolled right on over me. Nobody ever cared. It's a harsh reality that I had to learn. Now I want to teach that lesson to other people."

The vengeance in his voice made nausea roil in her stomach. "You need help, Dan."

"I tried to get help, and it didn't work!"

Sami needed to think of a different way to approach this, to figure out something that would get through to him. "But think about your wife, Amy. She's so sweet. What is she going to think if she finds out about this?"

His nostrils flared. "I don't want to hurt her. I'm sorry that it came down to this. But sometimes people have to learn lessons the hard way. Amy will figure things out on her own. She's a smart woman."

So Amy wasn't the key to calming him down right now . . . maybe Sami should dig deeper into his thought process. Maybe there was still part of him that was rational.

Maybe.

Sami remained frozen near the doorway. "What are you doing, Dan? Why did you go through all this trouble and bring me here?"

"Because we're going to finish what we started."

"And what did we start?"

"We had therapy sessions together. Now I want you to finish."

Sami nodded slowly, uncertain exactly how this

would play out. But at least she could buy some time. "Okay. Let's finish."

He raised his gun. "But every time you say something that disappoints me, there will be consequences. Painful consequences."

CHAPTER FORTY-ONE

BECKETT and his guys circled the small blue cottage where Dan's truck was parked.

They'd probably driven past the street before, but this house blended in with all the others. There was nothing special about it.

Right now, Beckett's team surrounded the building. On the count of three, they breeched the front door.

As Beckett stepped inside, he scanned everything around him.

It didn't look like anybody was here.

They searched the rest of the place only to confirm that it was empty.

His shoulders sagged with discouragement.

The team met back on the driveway.

Rocco turned to them. "There's one thing I noticed that's worth mentioning. I checked out his truck, and it doesn't appear the vehicle has been in an accident anytime recently."

"So he's on the island, but he's using a different vehicle and he's now at a different location," Beckett muttered. "Where else would he be?"

"That's what we need to figure out," Rocco said. "We're getting close. I can feel it."

Gabe stepped into the circle. "This guy is an engineer, right? And he does survey work."

"Right . . ." Beckett nodded.

Gabe nodded toward the sky. "Maybe he's done some survey work here on Lantern Beach. The only area that I can think where his services might be needed would be with either the lighthouse or maybe a new build. How many new builds are there on the island?"

"I can think of about five that are going up right now," Rocco said. "Do you think he might be at one of those places?"

"I think there's a good chance," Gabe said.

Beckett nodded back to their vehicles. "Then let's get busy. We have five properties to check out."

SAMI SAT down behind a desk and Dan stood in front of her, his gun resting in his hand on the table-top. She had no doubt he'd pull that trigger if he felt inclined.

"You think I'm going to shoot you, don't you?" he asked.

"Aren't you?"

He let out an empty laugh. "No. I'm going to shoot Ernie."

Her stomach sank. She had to figure out a way to stop this guy's rampage. "You don't want to do that, Dan."

"I'm tired of people telling me what I want to do and what I don't want to do! I'll be the judge of that."

Sami raised her hands in the air, desperate to calm him down. "Okay, okay. I get it. What do you want to talk about?"

She prayed she'd be able to find the right words. If she didn't, she wouldn't be the one who ended up hurt, and she couldn't stand the thought of that.

"Can you tell me where to start?"

She swallowed hard. "What happened when I started treating you? Can you tell me about it?"

"I was ten when I saw my mom die. She took pills, and I watched her life slip away right in front of me. I tried to save her, you know."

"I know you did."

"Then it was just me and my dad. He started taking me to see you. But what you didn't know was that when we were at home, he also started drinking to try to numb his pain."

"I'm sorry to hear that. I really am."

"In fact, he drank so much that the police ended up being called one night. I was put into foster care. Well, I suppose that's what you would call it. But no families would take me, so I ended up in a group home instead."

She swallowed hard as she heard the rage rising in his voice. "How did that go?"

"It was terrible. There were five other boys there with me, and I was the new guy. I was notably smaller than the rest of them, with less life experience. So I got bullied."

She heard the pain in his voice. "I'm sorry, Dan. I truly am. I can only imagine how hard that was."

With one hand, he wiped both his eyes. "It was. Then my dad went to go get treated for his alcoholism, but he didn't want me back. I think I reminded him too much of mom."

Her heart raced. "I see. But it seems like you still built a good life for yourself. You clearly went to college and did well. You have a beautiful wife. A good career."

"Maybe. They're the only things that keep me going."

"That's so important. To find something that makes you happy and to go for it. I think it's great that you rose above your circumstances."

He glanced around. "I did the survey work on this site."

Sami followed his gaze. That was why it was so dark in here. This place was a new build. The windows hadn't been cut out of the walls yet, and it appeared a tarp covered the exterior, probably because of the rain they'd had recently. That explained some of the situation.

"This project had actually been put on hold for a couple of weeks because of some finance issues," Dan explained. "So I decided that it might be good just to use this as my home base instead of the house I was staying at."

"You've always been smart."

"Why didn't you try to find me?" Any light disappeared from his eyes as he stared at her, his voice wavering with indignation.

"I did try to follow up a few times. But the system was stacked against me and . . ."

His nostrils flared. "That's the wrong answer, Dr. Reynolds."

He stood and stepped toward Ernie's room.

Panic raced through her and she jolted to her feet. "No, you can't do this!"

In one move, the gun hit her cheek.

She grasped her face as a throb began there.

He shook his head as he stared at her, something close to pity in his gaze.

"I *can* do this. And you're going to watch me."

CHAPTER FORTY-TWO

BECKETT and his guys had already searched two houses, but nobody was there. They were down to the last three.

When they pulled up to that third house, Lantern Beach PD with them, Beckett's gaze stopped at a truck that had been pulled into the trees and brush beside the house.

A dump truck.

Beckett strode toward it and pointed to the front of the vehicle. "Look at this, guys."

Several small dents were there, with streaks of paint matching the color of the car he'd been driving.

This was the vehicle used in the accident. It

suddenly made sense how the driver had hit them and been able to drive away.

"Most likely, they're inside this place." Beckett glanced up at the structure.

Like most homes in the area, it was on stilts. But the build was relatively new, and, although the walls were in place, no windows had been cut out yet.

A deck stretched in front of the entrance door, and a small stairway came down from the back.

The Blackout team—and police—would need to take both sides of the building and swarm the house to make sure that this guy didn't do anything stupid.

He prayed that Sami was okay.

Colton's gaze met the gaze of each of his team members. "Are we ready to do this?"

Beckett gripped his gun and nodded. "Let's get this over with."

Colton glanced at the police chief. "Chief Chambers, you're in charge."

"Let's do this," Cassidy said. "I'll call the shots from here while you guys do the footwork."

With nods to each other, the team surrounded the house.

As soon as Beckett reached the front door, Sami's voice came from inside.

"You don't want to do this, Dan." Terror filled her tone.

"Of course I do," a deeper voice said. "I wouldn't have come this far if I didn't want to do this."

"Dan . . . please. Put the gun down."

"No." Dan's voice hardened.

Then a bullet pierced the air.

Colton moved in front of Beckett, kicked the door in, and they flooded into the space.

SAMI GASPED when she heard a noise on the other side of the house.

Somebody was here.

But she couldn't afford to glance over.

Instead, she wrestled with Dan for the gun.

He'd just fired, but the bullet had hit the ceiling.

But next time, she and Ernie might not be so lucky.

"Put the gun down!"

She recognized that voice. It was Beckett. He'd found her. And he was okay.

Thank You, Jesus . . .

In an instant, Dan slipped the gun from her

grasp. One arm went around her neck and the other shoved the gun against her forehead.

She felt the blood drain from her face as she realized how precarious this situation was.

"You guys are the ones who need to put your guns down," Dan said. "If you don't, I'm going to shoot her."

"You don't want to do that." Beckett raised his hands before slowly placing his gun on the floor. The rest of his team followed suit.

"You found us faster than I thought you would," Dan said. "I don't know if I should give you an attaboy or if I should shoot you all."

"There's no need to shoot anybody," Beckett said. "Why don't we talk this through?"

"Because talking has gotten me nowhere. Talking has led me to this point."

"You don't want to hurt Sami," Beckett said. "She's kind. She wants to help you."

Sami nodded, sweat beading across her brow. "He's right. All I want to do is help people. The last thing I want to do is to fail anybody."

"Like you failed me?"

"It's clear that I did fail you, Dan. And I'm so sorry about that. Let me make it right. Let me get you help."

"I'm beyond help."

"I don't believe that," she said.

"I have nothing left to lose. My wife won't want anything to do with me when she finds out what I've done. I'll be thrown in jail if I am caught."

Nothing to lose? That didn't sound good. In fact, it sounded like the recipe for disaster.

As he shoved the metal barrel of the gun harder against Sami's forehead, she recoiled.

She had no doubt in her mind that Dan would pull the trigger. She was simply waiting for him to give in to the impulse.

CHAPTER FORTY-THREE

"CAN YOU PUT THE GUN DOWN?" Beckett stared at Dan, hoping to break through. "We can all talk about this. We can find a good solution."

"The only solution is if she dies," Dan growled, his nostrils flaring.

"Why is that the only solution?" Beckett stepped closer.

"Because Dr. Reynolds should have been there for me, and she wasn't."

"If you'd asked her for help, she would have given it to you," Beckett said. "I know Sami well enough to know that. She has a good heart."

"I shouldn't have to ask for help." The gun trembled in his hands.

"We all have to ask for help sometimes. There's

no shame in that. I've even had to ask for help on occasion myself."

Dan glanced at him. "But you were a Navy SEAL."

"Exactly. It doesn't matter how tough you are on the outside or on the inside. Sometimes, there are things that we can't work out on our own."

Dan stared at him a moment, and Beckett wondered if his words had worked.

Then anger filled the man's gaze again, almost as if a switch had flipped.

"You're just trying to get me to put the gun down." Dan's voice hardened again.

He must have pressed the gun into Sami because she let out a yelp.

Beckett's pulse raced even faster. "I do want you to put the gun down—because I don't want you to do anything you'll regret."

"How would you know what I would regret? You don't know anything about me."

Beckett locked his gaze on Dan's. "It's clear to see that you're hurting. Why don't you let us help?"

"Because it's too late for that," he growled.

Based on the look in Dan's eyes, he was about to do something very bad.

SAMI FELT Dan's heart racing faster as he pressed into her side.

She knew he was on the verge of ending her life.

She wasn't a fighter. Or a warrior.

Then again, Beckett wasn't a counselor, yet he was doing a tremendous job at trying to be one right now.

She'd been so wrong about him.

But there would be time to think more about that later.

Right now, she had to concentrate on surviving.

"What happened to you was wrong, Dan." Sami's voice wavered. "We can work to make sure that that doesn't happen to other people."

"You would do that, Dr. Reynolds?" A touch of surprise stretched through his words.

"Of course I would. He's telling the truth. I love my job. I love helping people. And just like with these guys—former SEALs—failure isn't an option when it comes to what I do."

He was silent a moment before snapping, "I don't believe you."

"I've never lied to you, Dan. I may have let you down, but I didn't lie." Sami needed to keep pushing forward before Dan convinced himself she wasn't telling the truth. "Dan, you deserve a much better life. People didn't do right by you. Including me. But you're a good person down deep inside. This isn't the way you want to work things out."

"I was left with no choice." An almost whining sound captured his words now. "Nobody would see me or hear me otherwise."

"Dan, you have the power to stop this. All you need to do is put down that gun."

"If I put down the gun, this is all over. They're going to shoot me."

"Their weapons are down," Sami reminded him. "They won't hurt you."

"Maybe I should just turn the gun on myself."

Her pulse quickened. "But then you wouldn't have a chance for redemption, to make things right."

"I don't want to go to jail." The whining sound increased.

"Dan, remember the story of King David."

"From the Bible?"

She nodded. "Yes, we read it together. Remember the horrible things he did?"

"He killed innocent people."

He remembered . . . good. "Exactly," Sami said. "But he still found redemption. Just like you can."

Tears ran down his face, and, for a moment, he reminded Sami of the teen she'd counseled.

"Give me the gun, Dan."

He stared at her a moment before lowering the weapon. Sami took it from him and placed it well out of reach on the table as the police took him into custody.

Beckett reached her just as her knees went weak. He caught her before she dropped to the floor.

It could have turned out so much differently, she realized. So, so much differently.

CHAPTER FORTY-FOUR

THE NEXT SEVERAL hours were a blur.

The FBI had arrived on scene and taken over.

Dan had been arrested.

Ernie had been taken to the clinic for treatment. He appeared to be okay—just shaken and dehydrated.

Currently, Sami sat with a blanket around her shoulders on the tailgate of one of the Blackout trucks. The blanket wasn't because she was cold. It was simply for comfort.

The Blackout crew was still on the scene, and the FBI was getting their statements.

Sami had been given permission to leave, but she wasn't ready to do that yet.

She still had too many things racing through her head. Too much had happened.

She'd almost lost her life . . . again.

She shivered.

What a wakeup call.

She could try to deny it all she wanted, but events like these changed a person's life. Made them reevaluate. Reprioritize.

Sami was no exception. Life was precious and not to be taken for granted. What did she really want for her future? Was the current track for her life where she wanted to head?

Even though she asked herself those questions, she already knew the answers.

Police Chief Chambers left one of the FBI agents she'd been speaking with and wandered to Sami. "How are you, Sami?"

"I'm grateful to be alive." Sami pulled the blanket closer. "Thank you for everything you've done."

Cassidy frowned. "I wish I could have done more. These guys at Blackout were really the ones who stepped up and put this all together."

"Yes, they were." She smiled when she remembered how brave they'd been.

She'd lived out her very own action movie, complete with handsome Navy SEALs.

Now she was ready to resume her old, boring life.

Kind of.

Not really, though.

"How's Annabeth?" Sami had helped evaluate a mute girl who'd been found here on the island a couple of months ago and had worked with Cassidy in the process.

"We still talk every week," Cassidy said. "She's doing really well."

"I'm so happy to hear that. And how's the baby?" She nodded at Cassidy's growing belly.

Cassidy's hand went to her abdomen, and her cheeks glowed, even in the dim lighting. "Doing fine. The morning sickness is starting to pass, thank goodness."

"I'm so excited for you."

"Thank you." Cassidy's expression turned serious. "I just thought I'd let you know that Dan has confessed to everything."

"The guy had a psychotic break." Sami frowned. She hadn't stopped thinking about it since being rescued. "I know it sounds strange, but I actually feel badly for him—and for his wife, Amy, also."

"That's understandable. That's what makes you so good at your job. You see beyond the surface."

"I'm very blessed to be able to do a job I love." Sami shifted and readjusted her blanket. "One question that's been bugging me. Where did Dan get those Dobermans? I would have seen the dogs if he'd had them at his house."

"Right before we were called to this scene, we got a notice that they'd been stolen from a home in Raleigh. The owner breeds Dobermans. Dan must have somehow found out about that and taken the dogs. They're trained to guard, and he somehow got them to attack." Cassidy shook her head and shrugged. "Dan . . . he's a smart man."

"That's what made him even scarier." Sami let out a long breath, so thankful this was over.

Before they could talk more, a figure appeared in the background.

Sami's breath hitched when she caught sight of those familiar broad shoulders.

Beckett.

She had to stop herself from running toward him and throwing her arms around his neck. But she'd never been so happy to see someone. She was so, so glad he was okay. So thankful for all he'd done. So enamored with the person she'd discovered him to be.

"I'll let you two have a moment." Cassidy nodded and joined her other officers in the distance.

As she stepped away, Beckett slowly strode toward her, his hands in his pockets and an unreadable expression on his face. Caution? Maybe. Weary? Possibly.

She just wasn't sure.

But she did know how she felt about him, and she needed to make that clear. She needed to swallow her pride and tell him that she'd been wrong. That she'd been trying to hide behind her protective walls. That she couldn't let fear hold her back.

Sami licked her lips, unsure how to even start this conversation.

"I'm so glad you're okay." The words seemed like a good place to start.

Beckett stepped closer, his warm eyes on her. "Me too. That was close back there."

"Good job talking to Dan. I think that really helped with that entire situation." Sami nibbled on her bottom lip. These things were important to say. But she knew she was avoiding what they really needed to talk about.

He shrugged. "I tried to put myself in his shoes."

"You're a remarkable man, Beckett Jones." Her

throat burned as she said the words. She meant every word. She just hoped it wasn't too late to make things right.

"And you're a remarkable woman."

She smiled at his words before swallowing deeply. "Thank you."

Thank you? She really needed to do better than that. It wasn't like her to feel so speechless.

"I've been thinking a lot about what you said when we talked earlier, before this mess happened," Beckett started.

"And?"

He reached for her and took her hand into his.

As he did, Sami felt the electricity zing through her.

"I was also thinking about my former job as a Navy SEAL," Beckett started. "Sometimes, my team has a battle plan and we do our best to prepare. But other times, while in the heat of the fight, we realize there's a better way and that sticking to our plan isn't the best."

She nodded slowly as his words sunk in. "I hear what you're saying."

His gaze locked onto hers. "Look, Sami, if you see things in me that you don't like, then by all means step back. But don't stay away from a potential relationship because you're afraid of getting hurt. Playing it by the book is a great way to protect yourself . . . but when you live life to the fullest, you can't always play it safe."

She squeezed his hand. "I'm thinking maybe you chose the wrong career. Maybe you should consider being a therapist."

Amusement glinted in his gaze. "Only if I'm allowed to give advice like, 'Suck it up, buttercup.'"

Sami smiled, but the motion faded as the weight of this conversation pressed on her. There were things she had to say to him as well. She had to explain herself, and she prayed she would have the right words.

"Beckett, you're right. I was scared. I wanted to protect my heart, and I thought following all the rules would allow me to do that. But when I let myself lower my guard and listen to my gut, I can't deny that you're everything I could ever want—and need."

His eyes warmed. "You mean that?"

She licked her lips, feeling unusually warm— and it wasn't because of the weather. "I do. I don't know what that means for us. My life is back in Atlanta but . . ."

"But what?"

"But I've also fallen in love with this island."

"It's a pretty great place."

She glanced around the weathered landscape surrounding this place—the dune grass, the sandy ground, the crushed seashells. "As a psychologist, I don't know what I'd do here. There are still a lot of things I need to figure out."

"We can figure things out. Together."

Together? It was refreshing to know she didn't have to find these solutions all alone. The thought of having someone to help carry her burdens already made her feel lighter. "I like the sound of that."

"Me too."

Her thoughts continued to race, to try to rationalize what was happening. The quality was innate—even in situations where her intuition told her differently. "I never expected to fall for someone this quickly. Honestly, it defies logic. It's—"

Beckett tucked a strand of hair behind her ear as he gazed at her. "A gift. That's what it is."

Sami's smile returned again. He was absolutely right. "Yes, it is a gift. You're a gift, Beckett Jones. And I'm okay if you save your smile only for me."

The ends of his lips curled as he leaned toward her. "I'm glad you give me something to smile about."

He wrapped his hands around her waist as he planted a kiss on her lips . . . one of many more to come.

~~~

Thank you so much for reading *Beckett*. If you enjoyed this book, please consider leaving a review!

COMING SOON: GABE

ALSO BY CHRISTY BARRITT:

LANTERN BEACH MYSTERIES

Hidden Currents

You can take the detective out of the investigation, but you can't take the investigator out of the detective. A notorious gang puts a bounty on Detective Cady Matthews's head after she takes down their leader, leaving her no choice but to hide until she can testify at trial. But her temporary home across the country on a remote North Carolina island isn't as peaceful as she initially thinks. Living under the new identity of Cassidy Livingston, she struggles to keep her investigative skills tucked away, especially after a body washes ashore. When local police bungle the murder investigation, she can't resist stepping in. But

Cassidy is supposed to be keeping a low profile. One wrong move could lead to both her discovery and her demise. Can she bring justice to the island . . . or will the hidden currents surrounding her pull her under for good?

Flood Watch

The tide is high, and so is the danger on Lantern Beach. Still in hiding after infiltrating a dangerous gang, Cassidy Livingston just has to make it a few more months before she can testify at trial and resume her old life. But trouble keeps finding her, and Cassidy is pulled into a local investigation after a man mysteriously disappears from the island she now calls home. A recurring nightmare from her time undercover only muddies things, as does a visit from the parents of her handsome ex-Navy SEAL neighbor. When a friend's life is threatened, Cassidy must make choices that put her on the verge of blowing her cover. With a flood watch on her emotions and her life in a tangle, will Cassidy find the truth? Or will her past finally drown her?

Storm Surge

A storm is brewing hundreds of miles away, but its effects are devastating even from afar. Laid-back, loose, and light: that's Cassidy Livingston's new motto. But when a makeshift boat with a bloody cloth inside washes ashore near her oceanfront home, her detective instincts shift into gear . . . again. Seeking clues isn't the only thing on her mind—romance is heating up with next-door neighbor and former Navy SEAL Ty Chambers as well. Her heart wants the love and stability she's longed for her entire life. But her hidden identity only leads to a tidal wave of turbulence. As more answers emerge about the boat, the danger around her rises, creating a treacherous swell that threatens to reveal her past. Can Cassidy mind her own business, or will the storm surge of violence and corruption that has washed ashore on Lantern Beach leave her life in wreckage?

Dangerous Waters

Danger lurks on the horizon, leaving only two choices: find shelter or flee. Cassidy Livingston's new identity has begun to feel as comfortable as her favorite sweater. She's been tucked away on Lantern Beach for weeks, waiting to testify against a deadly gang, and is settling in to a new life she wants to last forever. When she thinks she spots someone malevolent from her past, panic swells inside her. If an enemy has found her, Cassidy won't be the only one who's a target. Everyone she's come to love will also be at risk. Dangerous waters threaten to pull her into an overpowering chasm she may never escape. Can Cassidy survive what lies ahead? Or has the tide fatally turned against her?

Perilous Riptide

Just when the current seems safer, an unseen danger emerges and threatens to destroy everything. When Cassidy Livingston finds a journal hidden deep in the recesses of her ice cream truck, her curiosity kicks into high gear. Islanders suspect that Elsa, the journal's owner, didn't die accidentally. Her final entry indicates their suspicions might be correct and that what Elsa observed on her final night may have led to her demise. Against the advice of Ty Chambers, her former Navy SEAL boyfriend, Cassidy taps into her detective skills and hunts for answers. But her search only leads to a skeletal body and trouble for both of them. As helplessness threatens to drown her, Cassidy is desperate to turn back time. Can Cassidy find what she needs to navigate the perilous situation? Or will the riptide surrounding her threaten everyone and everything Cassidy loves?

Deadly Undertow

The current's fatal pull is powerful, but so is one detective's will to live. When someone from Cassidy Livingston's past shows up on Lantern Beach and warns her of impending peril, opposing currents collide, threatening to drag her under. Running would be easy. But leaving would break her heart. Cassidy must decipher between the truth and lies, between reality and deception. Even more importantly, she must decide whom to trust and whom to fear. Her life depends on it. As danger rises and answers surface, everything Cassidy thought she knew is tested. In order to survive, Cassidy must take drastic measures and end the battle against the ruthless gang DH-7 once and for all. But if her final mission fails, the consequences will be as deadly as the raging undertow.

LANTERN BEACH ROMANTIC SUSPENSE

Tides of Deception

Change has come to Lantern Beach: a new police chief, a new season, and . . . a new romance? Austin Brooks has loved Skye Lavinia from the moment they met, but the walls she keeps around her seem impenetrable. Skye knows Austin is the best thing to ever happen to her. Yet she also knows that if he learns the truth about her past, he'd be a fool not to run. A chance encounter brings secrets bubbling to the surface, and danger soon follows. Are the life-threatening events plaguing them really accidents . . . or is someone trying to send a deadly message? With the tides on Lantern Beach come deception and lies. One question remains—who will be swept away as the water shifts? And will it bring the end for Austin and Skye, or merely the beginning?

Shadow of Intrigue

For her entire life, Lisa Garth has felt like a supporting character in the drama of life. The designation never bothered her—until now. Lantern Beach, where she's settled and runs a popular restaurant, has boarded up for the season. The slower pace leaves her with too much time alone. Braden Dillinger came to Lantern Beach to try to heal. The former Special Forces officer returned from battle with invisible scars and diminished hope. But his recovery is hampered by the fact that an unknown enemy is trying to kill him. From the moment Lisa and Braden meet, danger ignites around them, and both are drawn into a web of intrigue that turns their lives upside down. As shadows creep in, will Lisa and Braden be able to shine a light on the peril around them? Or will the encroaching darkness turn their worst nightmares into reality?

Storm of Doubt

A pastor who's lost faith in God. A romance writer who's lost faith in love. A faceless man with a deadly obsession. Nothing has felt right in Pastor Jack Wilson's world since his wife died two years ago. He hoped coming to Lantern Beach might help soothe the ragged edges of his soul. Instead, he feels more alone than ever. Novelist Juliette Grace came to the island to hide away. Though her professional life has never been better, her personal life has imploded. Her husband left her and a stalker's threats have grown more and more dangerous. When Jack saves Juliette from an attack, he sees the terror in her gaze and knows he must protect her. But when danger strikes again, will Jack be able to keep her safe? Or will the approaching storm prove too strong to withstand?

Winds of Danger

Wes O'Neill is perfectly content to hang with his friends and enjoy island life on Lantern Beach.

Something begins to change inside him when Paige Henderson sweeps into his life. But the beautiful newcomer is hiding painful secrets beneath her cheerful facade. Police dispatcher Paige Henderson came to Lantern Beach riddled with guilt and uncertainties after the fallout of a bad relationship. When she meets Wes, she begins to open up to the possibility of love again. But there's something Wes isn't telling her—something that could change everything. As the winds shift, doubts seep into Paige's mind. Can Paige and Wes trust each other, even as the currents work against them? Or is trouble from the past too much to overcome?

Rains of Remorse

A stranger invades her home, leaving Rebecca Jarvis terrified. Above all, she must protect the baby growing inside her. Since her estranged husband died suspiciously six months earlier, Rebecca has been determined to depend on no one but herself. Her chivalrous new neighbor appears to be an answer to prayer. But who is Levi Stoneman really? Rebecca wants to believe he can help her, but she can't ignore her instincts. As danger closes in, both Rebecca and Levi must figure out whom they can trust. With Rebecca's baby coming soon, there's no time to waste. Can the truth prevail . . . or will remorse overpower the best of intentions?

Torrents of Fear

The woman lingering in the crowd can't be Allison . . . can she? Because Allison was pronounced dead six years ago. Musician Carter Denver knows only one person who's capable of helping him find answers: Sadie Thompson, his estranged best friend and someone who also knew Allison. He needs to know if he's losing his mind or if Allison could have survived her car accident. Could Allison really be alive? If so, why is she trying to harm Carter and Sadie? As the two try to find answers, can Sadie keep her feelings for Carter hidden? Could he ever care for her, or is the man of her dreams still in love with the woman now causing his nightmares?

LANTERN BEACH PD

On the Lookout

When Cassidy Chambers accepted the job as police chief on Lantern Beach, she knew the island had its secrets. But a suspicious death with potentially far-reaching implications will test all her skills

—and threaten to reveal her true identity. Cassidy enlists the help of her husband, former Navy SEAL Ty Chambers. As they dig for answers, both uncover parts of their pasts that are best left buried. Not everything is as it seems, and they must figure out if their John Doe is connected to the secretive group that has moved onto the island. As facts materialize, danger on the island grows. Can Cassidy and Ty discover the truth about the shadowy crimes in their cozy community? Or has darkness permanently invaded their beloved Lantern Beach?

Attempt to Locate

A fun girls' night out turns into a nightmare when armed robbers barge into the store where Cassidy and her friends are shopping. As the situation escalates and the men escape, a massive manhunt launches on Lantern Beach to apprehend the dangerous trio. In the midst of the chaos, a potential foe asks for Cassidy's help. He needs to find his sister who fled from the secretive Gilead's Cove community on the island. But the more Cassidy learns about the seemingly untouchable group, the more her unease grows. The pressure to solve both cases continues to mount. But as the gravity of the situation rises, so does the danger. Cassidy is deter-

mined to protect the island and break up the cult . . .
but doing so might cost her everything.

First Degree Murder

Police Chief Cassidy Chambers longs for a break
from the recent crimes plaguing Lantern Beach. She
simply wants to enjoy her friends' upcoming
wedding, to prepare for the busy tourist season
about to slam the island, and to gather all the dirt
she can on the suspicious community that's invaded
the town. But trouble explodes on the island,
sending residents—including Cassidy—into a squall
of uneasiness. Cassidy may have more than one
enemy plotting her demise, and the collateral
damage seems unthinkable. As the temperature
rises, so does the pressure to find answers. Someone
is determined that Lantern Beach would be better
off without their new police chief. And for Cassidy,
one wrong move could mean certain death.

Dead on Arrival

With a highly charged local election consuming
the community, Police Chief Cassidy Chambers
braces herself for a challenging day of breaking up
petty conflicts and tamping down high emotions.
But when widespread food poisoning spreads

among potential voters across the island, Cassidy smells something rotten in the air. As Cassidy examines every possibility to uncover what's going on, local enigma Anthony Gilead again comes on her radar. The man is running for mayor and his cult-like following is growing at an alarming rate. Cassidy feels certain he has a spy embedded in her inner circle. The problem is that her pool of suspects gets deeper every day. Can Cassidy get to the bottom of what's eating away at her peaceful island home? Will voters turn out despite the outbreak of illness plaguing their tranquil town? And the even bigger question: Has darkness come to stay on Lantern Beach?

Plan of Action

A missing Navy SEAL. Danger at the boiling point. The ultimate showdown. When Police Chief Cassidy Chambers' husband, Ty, disappears, her world is turned upside down. His truck is discovered with blood inside, crashed in a ditch on Lantern Beach, but he's nowhere to be found. As they launch a manhunt to find him, Cassidy discovers that someone on the island has a deadly obsession with Ty. Meanwhile, Gilead's Cove seems to be imploding. As danger heightens, federal law enforcement officials are called in. The cult's growing threat could lead to the pinnacle standoff of good versus evil. A clear plan of action is needed or the results will be devastating. Will Cassidy find Ty in time, or will she face a gut-wrenching loss? Will Anthony Gilead finally be unmasked for who he really is and be brought to justice? Hundreds of innocent lives are at stake . . . and not everyone will come out alive.

LANTERN BEACH BLACKOUT

Dark Water

Colton Locke can't forget the black op that went terribly wrong. Desperate for a new start, he moves to Lantern Beach, North Carolina, and forms Blackout, a private security firm. Despite his hero status, he can't erase the mistakes he's made. For the past year, Elise Oliver hasn't been able to shake the feeling that there's more to her husband's death than she was told. When she finds a hidden box of his personal possessions, more questions—and suspicions—arise. The only person she trusts to help her is her husband's best friend, Colton Locke. Someone wants Elise dead. Is it because she knows too much? Or is it to keep her from finding the truth? The Blackout team must uncover dark secrets hiding beneath seemingly still waters. But those very secrets might just tear the team apart.

Safe Harbor

Guilt over past mistakes haunts former Navy SEAL Dez Rodriguez. When he's asked to guard a pop star during a music festival on Lantern Beach, he's all set for what he hopes is a breezy assignment. Bree hasn't found fame to be nearly as fulfilling as she dreamed. Instead, she's more like a carefully crafted character living out a pre-scripted story. When a stalker's threats become deadly, her life—and career—are turned upside down. From the start, Bree sees her temporary bodyguard as a player, and Dez sees Bree as a spoiled rich girl. But when they're thrown together in a fight for survival, both must learn to trust. Can Dez protect Bree—and his carefully guarded heart? Or will their safe harbor ultimately become their death trap?

Ripple Effect

Griff McIntyre never expected his ex-wife and three-year-old daughter to come to Lantern Beach. After an abduction attempt, they're desperate for safety. Now Griff's not letting either of them out of his sight. Bethany knows Griff is the only one who can protect them, despite the fact that he broke her heart. But she'll do anything to keep her daughter safe—even if it means playing nicely with a man she can't stand. As peril ripples through their lives, Griff and Bethany must work together to protect their daughter. But an unseen enemy wants something from them . . . and will stop at nothing to get it. When disaster strikes, can Griff keep his family safe? Or will past mistakes bring the ultimate failure?

Rising Tide

Benjamin James knows there's a traitor within his former command. The rest of his team might even think it's him. As danger closes in, he must clear himself and stop a deadly plot by a dangerous terrorist group. All CJ Compton wanted was a new start after her career ended under suspicion. Working as the house manager for private security group Blackout seems perfect. But there's more trouble here than what she left behind. As the tide rushes in, the stakes continue to rise. If the Blackout team fails, it's not just Lantern Beach at stake—it's the whole country. Can Benjamin and CJ overcome their differences and work together to find the truth?

ABOUT THE AUTHOR

USA Today has called Christy Barritt's books "scary, funny, passionate, and quirky."

Christy writes both mystery and romantic suspense novels that are clean with underlying messages of faith. Her books have won the Daphne du Maurier Award for Excellence in Suspense and Mystery, have been twice nominated for the Romantic Times Reviewers' Choice Award, and have finaled for both a Carol Award and Foreword Magazine's Book of the Year.

She is married to her Prince Charming, a man who thinks she's hilarious—but only when she's not trying to be. Christy is a self-proclaimed klutz, an avid music lover who's known for spontaneously bursting into song, and a road trip aficionado.

When she's not working or spending time with her family, she enjoys singing, playing the guitar, and exploring small, unsuspecting towns where people have no idea how accident-prone she is.

Find Christy online at:
   www.christybarritt.com
   www.facebook.com/christybarritt
   www.twitter.com/cbarritt

Sign up for Christy's newsletter to get information on all of her latest releases here: **www. christybarritt.com/newsletter-sign-up/**

If you enjoyed this book, please consider leaving a review.

Made in the USA
Las Vegas, NV
24 October 2024